BLOO

MIS

NAYLOR

BLOODING MISTER NAYLOR
is a political thriller cum whodunnit set in the "New" Glasgow. A peace camper is accused of murdering a veteran left-wing nationalist. Jackie Naylor, the peace campers' lawyer, is called in to defend him. But Naylor, an ex-captain in Army Intelligence, has been sending reports to the Ministry of Defence on the campers' activities. He finds himself abandoned by his masters and drawn into a whirl-pool of double dealing and violence. Christopher Boyce is Scottish. His previous fiction has been science fiction novels and stories. His most recent story, BIRTHPLACE, was nominated for a Nebula award by the Science Fiction writers of America. He writes on computer science and spaceflight for the Glasgow Herald. His novels are: CATCHWORLD, which won the 1974 Sunday Times SF Novel competition and was nominated for a Nebula award; and BRAINFIX. Non-fiction: EXTRATERRESTRIAL ENCOUNTERS: a personal perspective.

BLOODING MISTER NAYLOR

by

CHRIS BOYCE

DOG AND BONE
GLASGOW 1990

THIS NOVEL WAS
FIRST PUBLISHED
IN 1990 SCOTLAND
BY
DOG & BONE
PRESS
175 QUEEN VICTORIA
DRIVE, GLASGOW
DESIGNED BY
ALASDAIR GRAY
TYPESET BY
DONALD SAUNDERS
PRINTED, BOUND
BY
COX & WYMAN,
CARDIFF RD, READING

ISBN 1 872536 04 2

for the Angel of Dunkenny Square
with love and admiration.

AUTHOR'S DISCLAIMER
The names of real people appear in the
following text but none of the characters is real or intended to represent a
real person. The Glen Douglas peace
camp is imaginary and not to be confused with the Faslane peace camp and
its admirable dedicated inhabitants
(that includes Sam) – more power to
their elbow.

The attitudes and language
expressed in this book may offend
some people. I am not sorry for that. It
is based on the city and the people
I know. It is partisan and so am I.

TABLE OF CONTENTS

Life's a bitch and then you die ...
— Street wisdom, Glasgow 1990

One:Toccata

MUCH MUCH LATER, when the repercussions had totally reshaped his lifeplan, Naylor would work out where he was, what he was doing at the exact moment they murdered the old woman. A Friday afternoon in the tail end of August around half four, Naylor was in his Nova Cabriolet zooming west along the Dumbarton Road. Destination the Dumbuck Hotel and Blitz night.

Analysing that day he realised there had been plenty portents of disaster. Over breakfast the Radio Clyde astrologer had been blunt – the cosmos was ganging up on him. Immediately the pronouncement was given the coffee grinder died, condemning him to choose between instant, which he detested, and the box of lapsong suchong teabags kept solely to impress any female who might cross his portal. He tried the tea, decided it was like drinking hot water from a used ashtray and dumped it down the sink. The Nova had started acting up the second he turned the key. He ground his teeth really really hard. How could an almost new car which was running smooth as the proverbial baby's buttock when parked the night before have contracted what sounded like a major pulmonary infection just sitting there doing utter bugger all in the lock-up? Eh? Eh?

But the real blazing sign in the heavens had been Forbes. Sheriff Peter 'Kermit' Forbes had been on the bench, leaning slightly forward with both arms angled on the desk before him, ogling the court's occupants, particularly the accused and the defence agents, with a watery animosity. He reminded Naylor for all the world of a kind of refugee from a wildlife programme like a Nepalese tree frog or something. He had a sole redeeming quality in the form of a singularly attractive niece. Naylor entertained designs upon this young woman's marital status. Apart from being the daughter of an MP and having the frog king for an uncle she was classically well heeled and passably pretty. The latter aspect did not come from the Forbes side of her family. She lacked the rheumily active amphibian eyes. As they alighted on Naylor, gowned and wrestling with a file-crammed briefcase, he experienced a feeling rather akin to stepping into a bathtub of cold greasy water. He sensed that extremely unpleasant things were about to happen to his clients. Happen they did.

That morning Naylor had been appearing for two peace-campers. Their forte was lying across the road in the path of large army vehicles which they claimed were transporting nuclear warheads. This trick they had performed once more with customary abandon.

There had been ample media cover the night before. Newspersons of all conceivable varieties had wrung every last vestige of a story from the situation and with the case over they would happily toss it away and move onto something fresh. Not that the peace-campers cared. To them this was an engineered opportunity to put their case (the one against all things nuclear) to the press and broadcasting media. Or so they hoped. They pled guilty and when asked if they had anything to say for themselves went rabbiting on about everything from the ozone layer to the latest attempt at forcing them to pay rates. The sheriff turned to salt. The press turned and ran. None of their sentiments, never mind actual words, would appear in print or be reported on the box. Forbes had handed out fifty quid fines apiece.

Wonderful. It almost put Naylor off lunch.

The only opportunity for some mileage would have been if the press had waited to interview Naylor himself leaving the Sheriff Court.

No such luck. The afternoon had seen a procession of the impoverished trail through his office doors. This had set him wondering again why Munro Kerr Meikle, one of Glasgow's most upper crust law firms, should want to open up a legal aid practice in Dumbarton. Certainly it made money enough to pay himself and Bobby Turner his assistant. More importantly it also paid Ann Burns his secretary, coffee maker, taker of precognitions and general amanuensis. It even turned out a profit of a few grand a year for the company coffers. But he suspected the real reason for its existence was cosmetic. MKM liked to appear not only to possess a broad range of legal skills but also to have 'social awareness.' All part of the corporate image. And these days Glasgow was all corporate image.

The fact they knew that the Ministry of Defence put the odd backhander Naylor's way to clipe on the peace-campers made him wonder what the real face of MKM was like under all that cosmetic.

But he only wondered occasionally.

Awaiting his return at the office were were two fresh bruised wife beatees pursuing divorces, a child custody where two drunks were fighting over the life of nine year old now showing signs of a budding but virulent psychosis and finally there was a woman who wanted to sue Channel Four for infesting her water with television waves which were making her house stink.

What was so very irritating about them was the fact he invariably became enmeshed with their lives, engrossed in what he regarded as being the social dross of his world. There were even times he lost sleep over them. Once or twice a year he would resolve not to go overboard on their cases. Such resolutions had all the rigour of a tub of butter on a hot sunny day. God help him, he even *liked* some of them!

The office closed at four on Fridays. For this he was profoundly grateful. Before he left the office Anne Burns phoned a local chippie and ordered a special fish supper and a pickled egg for him to pick up on his way home. This he devoured with a couple of slices of buttered bread in the dining kitchen of his Young Executive Studio Flat in Clydebank.

He now understood that a 'studio flat' meant the flat had one room, an 'executive' version meant it had a separate kitchen and 'young' meant it was the smallest available. When drinking cohort Paul Goldman had seen it he had wheezed with laughter cautioning Naylor not to inhale too deeply in case he sucked the Anaglypta off the walls.

Naylor almost liked the flat. It looked good from the outside, part of a new housing development faced with wee bricks raised in knitting patterns and looking terribly sub

sub Charles Rennie MacIntosh. He felt it went well with the white Nova Cabriolet. It would obviously have been better to live in a converted warehouse as was fashionable in New York and London. Trouble was finding an abandoned warehouse to convert. In the Glasgow conurbation they tended to burn down.

The good thing about Friday nights was the bad thing about Saturday mornings: the evening was usually spent in the bar of the Dumbuck Hotel. Blitz night! Yaaaay!

This tradition had persisted since his Army days. One night at the weekend set aside for major brain damage. Problem was finding other like minded individuals of one's station in civvy life. There were plenty of solid drinkers but they tended to be at least five years younger than Naylor, usually more. You could tell when they married; at first they'd just go home earlier; eventually they'd make only the rarest of appearances; then in some cases they popped up in spasmodic bursts and rapidly began spending every night in the bar. The latter cases were heading for divorce and the wonderful world of alcoholism.

The exception was Paul Goldman. As Naylor pulled into the car park of the Dumbuck he frowned. No sign of the Goldman Maestro.

Normally its metallic grey lines were to be seen in the hotel environs a good quarter hour before Naylor's arrival.

The bar was cluttered with solicitors, fiscals and Sheriff Clerks. These were the married ones, the hubbies. In for their one hour pub time before tearing back to the little woman and the kiddiewinks.

A few raised their hands or glasses in acknowledgement. He nodded back. A few others exchanged flashes of distaste. This satisfied Naylor. Gratifying to know one was working one's way right up certain nostrils. When he was a boy soldier his drill master had emphasised life was not a general popularity contest; all you had to know was those few people it was necessary to impress – the rest could go inseminate themselves!

Settled into a corner of the bar from which he could readily see the door, he charged the first of his treble vodkas with tonic and prepared to suffer fools with generous gladness until Goldman arrived.

The 'Phone for you Mr Naylor' came at around twenty to six with the first sip just taken from the third treble and already a mist of sparkling well-being suffusing all corners of the known universe.

'Jack, do you ever work?' It was the voice of the absent Goldman. 'I must've phoned your office half a dozen times between quarter past four and five. Easily!'

'We groom the horses between four and five on Fridays. I take it this call signifies you're chickening out on this evening's thermonuclear exchange?'

'Sister's arrived from London with her two weans. That arse-face she married came out the closet and ran off with a man on Wednesday. She's simmering away on the edge of hysteria. No way am I going to make it tonight, old son.'

'I am cursed with a bad day. This is a bad bad day.'

'Look. Can you come over here? Get a carry out. Couple of bottles. That Russian vodka you eat and a Glenlivet forty ouncer for her and me?'

'Christ, drive all the way out to Rhu? For a few drinkies with you and your married sister? Run the gauntlet of the Dumbarton bloody police. Those boys are out for my skin, by the way. This has turned into one dirty big jobby of a day.'

'Oh, I see we're talking excrement already. By my reckoning that puts you into your third treble, Jack.'

'Approximately.'

'Listen. Why don't you come out here tomorrow afternoon, early if possible. We can all go for a sail and have a nice meal down in Helensburgh in the evening. You stay over. Beth and I'll make up a room for you. Stay the weekend.'

'Mmmmmmmmmmm ...'

'And forget about getting pissed as a fart tonight. We can do that in style after dinner tomorrow. In fact come over really early and I'll chuck in a barbecue lunch as well.'

'Mmmmm. Yummy. Now you're talking Turkish, my boy!'

Paul said something about between one and two which Naylor almost missed because of a roar from a drinking scrum of off-field rugby players. When it lowered Paul had hung up. Naylor made his way back. His treble, a giant box of Swans, a packet of Castellas and an ashtray holding a lit cigar staking his territory at the bar.

The hubbies were now being replaced by a generally younger noisier crowd, the dedicated Friday night revellers, the true weekend alcoholics.

Looking back on it he would agree with himself that at this point he was ready to leave, to go home via Azad video, grab a couple of tapes and spend a restful night in front of the box eyeballing some soft porn. Instead another vodka materialised just as he belted down what he expected to be his last. He frowned at the supernatural manifestation. His last surprise drink had been bought by a dubious

Belgian while he was stationed in West Germany. That night a car bomb had been waiting for three of his mates in the parking lot. The dubious Belgian had vanished but the local cops very soon made links with the IRA. That was the night Naylor decided to divorce the Army.

'Good grief, Jack, it's just a drink. You'd think it was concentrated nitric acid from your face.' The voice had a singsong, almost camp Kelvinside intonation. Naylor winced and looked round.

Frank Lambie was almost upon Naylor when he clocked him. The fiscal was rigged out in a vast new Humphrey Bogart trenchcoat, a tall ship sailing through minor vessels with poise. One hand dropped on Naylor's shoulder with the vitality of a gutted fish. The other threw pound notes to the barmaid and scooped up a champagne cocktail which he raised to Naylor in a mock toast. They had gone through university together, Naylor an Army sponsored student doing his best to keep out of Ulster, Lambie a potential addition to the largest family legal practice in Ayrshire. Naylor, to no one's particular surprise had gone into the Army Intelligence Corps. Lambie to everyone's surprise had gone to the Crown Office.

'So how's life in the Big City, Frank? Cheers.'

'Oh, improving by degrees, Jack, by degrees,' he smirked, a gold masonic swivel ring glittering from one finger. 'I have to say being a Senior in Glasgow's much more challenging than being a Legal Assistant out here in the sticks. Stretches you, you know? But I really think that's what one has to do if one wants to get anywhere as a legal lifeform, don't you? I mean its like this book on criminal procedure in the Sheriff Court I've been commissioned, pseudonymously of course, to write with Peter Forbes. You know, the Sheriff.'

'Oh I do know.' What in the name of Mammon is a legal lifeform?

'But it's where am I going to find the time? What with increased workload and my new position with the golf club. Did you know I'm now Treasurer? Well, I suppose somebody has to do it, hmm? Oh, excuse me, dear! Excuse me! Another round here, please. Yes, same again. How does she remember all the drinks everyone orders? Anyway what have you been up to, Jack. Mmmmm? And a packet of crisps, dear! Have you any smoky bacon?'

'Well, of course business is booming, Frank. Booming. I'm talking to the senior partners about expanding the whole operation. It's becoming an absolute must now,' Naylor lied.

'Why can you just never get smoky bacon anywhere these days?'

'Mind you, I'm going to take a well deserved rest. Thinking of maybe a few weeks on Bali or maybe the Maldives?' Naylor did not even have to think about it; in the presence of the Lambies of this little world he went automatically into bullshit mode.

'Oh the Maldives every time, Jack. If I may make so bold there's one wee stoater of an island. Bandos. It's about the size of Hampden, circular. The ultimate in get-away-from-it-all and then some. I considered it for the honeymoon but I don't think she who must be obeyed much fancies any place without extremely fashionable shops, you know, the kind with the gazetteer at the end of their names; Paris, Berlin, Rome, New York. Tend to be something of a rarity on the remoter island paradises, if you follow my drift.' Lambie had a nice cache of family money in the bank and liked his peers to know it.

Naylor said, 'I'm developing an interest in polo.
Thought I might take my break at a polo school. Like to
find out if there's anyone else interested. You know, a few
of us could share costs on a string of polo ponies. How 'bout
you, Frank? Polo's your kind of thing.'

And so they talked polo for an hour. Naylor, in
drink, could appear plausible on any subject. In the Army,
after a detailed legal education, he'd culled a completely
general education by reading the entire 1973 revised four-
teenth edition of Encyclopaedia Britannica. This took
twelve years. Every subsequent year he read the
Encyclopaedia's World Data Annual to keep up to date. It
was something he never boasted about.

The source of information, one's intelligence, had
to be guarded at all costs. Any idiot knew that and Jack
Naylor was not just any idiot! No, talking polo was not the
problem. Talking was the problem. The words were
telescoping, colliding. In the toilet mirror he saw the scarlet
blush across neck and cheek that meant he was brain-fried.

He swayed back to Lambie at the bar. Lambie now
drinking white wine spritzers which looked like champagne
cocktails and had all the kick of a grasshopper.

'Jack,' said Lambie. 'I have to shoot off now but
I've just had a thought. I'm going along to a wee do at
Duntocher, meeting she who must be obeyed there. There'll
be a fair number of young lawyers. They might be quite
interested in your idea about the polo ponies. Fancy coming
along for a drink or two?'

'Drink? Sure know how to sweet talk a guy!'

They plunged through the rain in Lambie's silver
Saab. Naylor tried to remember if he had the soft top on the

Nova up or down but gave up trying to concentrate on anything so concrete. It was easier just to go along with the swish swosh of the wipers batting the rain from side to side and hum some Bach.

'What's that, Tina Turner?'

'JSB. Suite one in C. The Courante. Christ, you're uncultured, Frank. I mean you really are. And moving to the 1990 Euro Culture Capital too, eh? What a cheek! Mind you, lawyers are fairly uncultured as a genus. I mean really. They are. Last week. Chatting up this agent from Harper's Bizarre. Asked if she liked Kafka. Know what she said? Would you believe it? Would you? Says, "Oooo I never eat Greek food." Fuck a duck! What a maroon! Greek food.'

'Well, I have to agree with her, Jack. I find it a trifle oily for my palate. And the wines are a wee bitty rough edged. Lots of body, of course. Very loud. Mind you, wouldn't do if we all liked the same things.'

'I see you're a philosopher.'

'And so should you be, Jack. I mean you seem to take your cases so damned personally. Every time you lose even the most blatant of offenders to the arms of penal retribution. Well, what a face. Hangdog's not the word. Do you know you pout? Really pout? I'm not just being metaphorical. You actually stand there looking at the bench and the clerks and the fiscals with a petted lip, Jack. To be perfectly frank, if you'll excuse my wee pun, it's more or less unprofessional.'

'Hah. You mean the welly boot case? The one you followed around. I could hardly credit my eyes when I saw you out in the public benches that day. My God, you really wanted to see my man go down, eh? And he did too, for five years. And why? Cannabis found in a bloody welly boot!'

21

'Three and a half kilos of it.'

'Bench totally hostile – '

'Appeal it, Jack. This is what I mean. You take it all far too personally. As you say, I'm fairly philosophical. To me it's all a sport. A bit like game shooting. You should look at it that way too. Admittedly it's a bit of a blood sport but a sport nevertheless. And I think a good lawyer should be a good sport.'

One of the first cases the Dumbarton office had handled was drugs related. Naylor had done a good job of defending and the word soon spread. An increasing number of druggies came his way. Poor souls, lost souls all of them, the addict-dealers, thieves and prostitutes. Watching them go down was torment. The sweating white faces looked into his dreams. Something should be done, he thought, but the rehab facilities were inadequate for a country of more than a few hundred addicts, for a few hundred thousand they were a sour joke.

By the time the Saab was pulling into the Maltings Hotel car park the rain had trickled down to a damp drizzle. Enough for a clear view of the other vehicles standing at rest, sited for convenience and display; the Volvos, the Porches, the Mercedes and the BMWs and two bright red sports jobs, one Japanese, one Italian, both apparently built for space travel.

Naylor leaned forward, narrowed his eyes and said, 'She's here!'

'I beg your pardon? Have I much room on your side?' The Saab eased smoothly into place at the end of the line of cars.

'That's her Escort. One with all the weird lights and do dahs.'

'Oh, Mel Forbes. Yes. Believe she won some rally thingy the other day driving that wee monster. Over in Northern Ireland. Hmmph. More money than sense if you ask me.' Lambie reached across to the glove compartment and lifted out a Canon SureShot.

'*Mel?*' Naylor squeaked clambering from the car, slamming the door. 'Name's Melanie. Where d'you get this "Mel" crap?'

'Your shirt's hanging out the back. Tuck it in. There's a good chap. Oh, it's her nickname. Just used by her chums, of course.'

'Ho!' hooted Naylor, thrusting lilac gingham shirt into his grey cords as he caramboled a path through the crowded entrance. 'Suppose that makes you a "chum" then? Eh? One of Mel's Chums, eh? There a bar around here?'

Lambie tutted and sighed pulling him to one side of the door into the main lounge. He tried tidying the broad knotted burgandy tie at Naylor's neck. 'Did you leave your jacket in the car?'

'Naaa. Must be in the Dumbuck,' Naylor shrugged. 'S'okay-dokey. Got the drinking vouchers with me. Aaaaaaay!' Waving a fistful of five and ten pound notes over his head. Jumping and thumping his trainer clad heels together in the air. 'Taxi out there for lunchies tomorrow. Pick up jacket and car. Robert's the proverbial uncle. Where's this luscious Mizzzz Forbes then, that I may unzip my charms before her? I can say something like "Hello Mel – you're really swell!" Brill! It rhymes and everything!'

A little grim smile crossed Lambie's face staying just long enough for it to register dimly in a cranny of Naylor's mostly submerged mind. Then the fiscal piloted him towards the private function suite shedding the trenchcoat en route to reveal a splendid white tux and red bow tie.

Through the doors and heads turned. There were about three dozen of them all in dinner clothes. Naylor's powers of observation, slightly diminished, could still savour a mixture of facial expressions; among the males grins of merriment and shared wicked winks, among the females annoyance and distaste. And among the females the blonde princess, Melanie Forbes, looking yummy in a figure revealing black dress. She had made herself into a lookalike for Diana Frances Spencer the moment it had become obvious in early 1980 that said lady was to become consort to Charles, Duke of Rothesay and Prince of Wales.

How to sweep her off her feet? Naylor wondered chaotically.

He shouted across the room, 'Oh Mel. Oh Mel. I love your smell. What wonderful aroma. It drives me wild. It knocks me out. I think I'm in a coma!' And he flashed her what he felt was a conspiratorial but boyish smile. She held his eye for a moment. Twice he had dated this young woman, drank moderately, a model of impeccable manners, of gentle wit. She had laughed, responded. But tonight her face had all the tender warmth of a slightly curled haddock which would never leave the freezer. He sighed. Elsewhere, he knew, his efforts were appreciated; giggles, choked back laughter and more tuttings, more urgent female mutterings.

'Jack has this wonderful plan for buying polo ponies!' Lambie announced steering him into a shoal of barracuda smooth young men who bared their teeth with anticipation.

'Has he really? Fascinating.' It was that voice with the fully-fitted sneer Naylor could recognise anywhere. He turned and there on the other side of the small group, holding court, sat Sheriff Peter Forbes. 'Our second encounter of the day, Mr Naylor, and it does not appear as if you're going to come out of this one any better off than the first.'

There was a clutch of chuckles.

Naylor sank to his knees before the frog king, threw his arms wide and proclaimed, 'Your Royal Imperial Highness,' And bowed and straightened and added, 'Rivet-rivet! Rivet-rivet!'

He bayed with laughter and threw his head back and back it went, back and down, down through the depths to oblivion.

Two:Andante

BREEEEEBREEEEE … The phone could just be heard above the noise of the crowd in the empty room. God what a rammy! Why was Forbes riding around on a polo pony anyway? What the hell was Lambie doing jigging about in his white tux and masonic apron? And jigging with the fair Melanie all frosted and fishy …

Breeeeebreeeee …Why all these other fan-dancers in their dickey suits …And what were they doing in his flat?

Breeeeebreeeee …He fumbled the switch of the table lamp into the on position and swung legs off bed and torso up into quasi-sitting posture. This motion invested his brain with totally independent rotation within the cranium.

'Jee-zuz …'

Breeeeebreeeee …

'Comin.' I'm comin'.' Naylor rose and fell back to the crumpled bed and rose and made his way through the carousing phantasms to the wall with the ringing phone.

''S up?'

'Good morning, sir. Cranstonhill Police Station, Constable Carmichael speaking. Is that Mr John Naylor, solicitor?'

'Time's it?'

'Three minutes past six am, sir. That is Mr Naylor?'

'Right. Six in the morning? Christ Almighty.'

'Pardon, sir?'

'Nothin.' Er, what's the problem, officer?' Clearing throat.

Trying to sound professional, alert, totally in control of the ball. Riding a bike underwater.

'We have an Alan Banks in custody. Age thirty. And a Deborah Mooney aged twenty six. Both give their address as the Glen Douglas peace camp. They've been charged with murder and want you to represent them.'

'Murder?'

'Murder, sir.'

Naylor tried thinking about it in the shower. The heating was screwed up and the best temperature he could wring from it was tepid. He cursed and banged the plastic case of the control unit. The little red light flicked out. The water turned cold. Concentrates the mind wonderfully, like he decided. Just what we require on our first murder case. He withstood the freezing onslaught for all of three seconds and staggered out onto the lino, grappling for a towel, found a large one and wrestled in it for a few minutes until he was mainly dry.

Frowning, he loped back into the room. Did I go out last night? Calibrate the hangover: head inflating and contracting like a burning lung, mouth that tastes cesspit ripe. It was a fairly stupid question.

Pulling on fresh socks and underwear he had his first memory; Paul on the phone in the Dumbuck Hotel and some arrangement to meet for lunch later today. He smiled. Something about his sister. Good. He phoned Boulevard for a car. Asked if Harry was on. He wasn't. And he was cursing yet more bad luck when another memory broke the surface of consciousness like something unpleasant rising to the top of a bowl of soup: the Maltings.

'Oh no, please no, Lord.' He shook his head fiercely and had to sit quickly or fall over.

Do not think about last night. Leave it an unexplored territory. Must get out and see what this rubbish is about Banksie. No time for recrimination, or self pity or any other crap. Get to it, Naylor. Button up the coat and head-first into the hailstorm! C'mon, Jackie boy, you can do it.

Forty minutes after picking up the phone he was stepping through the cell door with the appearance of a sober, concerned professional, all wreckage sunk from sight. As Naylor entered the big man rose, his six foot three plus soaring an easy eight inches over the top of Naylor's head. Confusion and perhaps some panic had flushed his round face. The desk sized hands moved continuously, opening and closing, smoothing down the expanse of thick knit turtleneck which had once been deep purple but now passed for black. Pork sausage fingers plucked at the beard, ran through greasy curls of hair. A man, Naylor decided, almost out of control. So he held up a hand summoning silence until the door closed behind him.

'Mr Naylor, I – '

'Don't tell me if you did it! I don't want to know. I'm not interested in your guilt or your innocence. That's for the jury to decide. Right? I'm here to act on your behalf for whatever defence can be put before the court. I can arrange for a counsel and so on. But tell me you're guilty and want a defence and I'll have to withdraw. Okay?'

Amazingly his standard spiel had rolled out impeccably.

'Mr Naylor, I didn't do it. I didn't. Really.' The gentle Liverpudlian accent from this enormous beast always caught Naylor by surprise.

'Right, Alan, right. Let's sit down. Okay. Want a ciggy?'

Banks sat down slapping oaktree thighs bejeaned in faded denim, 'Y'know I never use the things, Mr Naylor.'

'Sorry, that's right. That's right. Now let's see – '

'But I'll try one anyway. Just this once. Anything to calm me nerves.' Naylor sat beside him, opened the briefcase and passed him a Stuyvesant, ignited it with his gunmetal Zippo. Banks took a long deep drag and sighed pale smoke. 'Not bad. Maybe I should've taken the weed up years ago?'

Tell me about it, Alan. They claim you murdered some woman called ...' He shuffled his notes, 'Yes, Pamela Alexandra Cairns or Beattie aged 83, of 20 St Vincent Crescent.'

'That's Lexie Beattie.'

'Lexie Beattie? You mean the CND woman, the nationalist left winger? That old dear?'

Banks nodded. 'That old dear. I was up seeing her earlier tonight, well, yesterday afternoon, really – '

'I didn't even know you knew her. Was she connected with the peace camp?'

'Well ... over the years she became quite involved, I suppose. She was good at drumming up support, y'know? She even ran our newsletter for a bit. Nothing ever seemed too much for the old soul.'

'What's your version of what happened yesterday?'

'Well, we were in town – '

'Who's "we"?'

'Oh er, Debs ... Debs Mooney and me. She took the van down to Asda. God knows why but she likes to shop there once a month for supplies. I went up to see Lexie. We've got a tricky operation on the cards right now, you see. If we can organise a big enough network of observers we'll finally be able to prove that NATO stores nuclear warheads in the Glen. I wanted some advice on setting this up. To be absolutely frank I wanted to use a lot of her contacts.'

'What time was this?'

'Oh, three to half past more or less.'

'And there was no argument?'

'Why should there be an argument? We went over the people she felt could help. I mean she had some great ideas, some absolutely unbelievable angles on things – .'

'When did you leave?'

'Maybe something like five, ten past four.'

'Uh-huh?'

'Well, then I went up to the Argyle Street corner. Y'know, the one that's all boarded up where the bank used to be and Debs turned up after maybe five minutes and d'you believe it she had this wimp she met in the bloody store says he wants to come and join us. Just like that. Well, we had a bit of a shout out. Y'know. I give her a bollicking. He buggers off smart like. I tell her to go screw herself and she hooks it in the van and I head into the nearest pub.'

'Which pub's that?'

'What's it called? The one on the corner cross the road from here? Bannisters.Anyway I just stay on in there guzzling heavy til it's chucking out time and who's waiting for me when I step outside? Boys in Blue. None other.

Must've been about twenty of them. And a van. You could tell they were really scared. Can't blame them. I'm a big lad. Lots of drink taken. Potentially hazardous.' He laughed, dropped the half smoked cigarette at his feet and mashed it under the sole of an army surplus boot.

'So this would be the back of eleven?'

'Nearer midnight. Then we just toddled over the road. Very handy having a cop shop next door to the scene of the crime.'

Naylor sighed and thought about it. Thinking engine's gears were near stripped but it chugged along. 'We better find someone who saw her after you left, Alan. And we better get our hands on that character Deborah picked up in Asda. Sorry, I'll rephrase that; the character she bumped into in Asda. When you went into that pub you were probably a wee bit upset. Angry. Right? So the cops'll include that in their evidence so it can be used against you. They'll ask around the pub for witnesses. Find out everything you said. This Asda character will be able to confirm there was an argument between you and Deborah. Was the meeting between you and Miss Beattie peaceful? Was there any shouting or what?'

'What would we shout about? Dear God, she was one of the ancients. She knew more about politics and I mean all kinds of politics than anyone we'd ever get a chance to talk to. We didn't argue with her. We listened to her advice and either we took it or we didn't. Usually we took it.'

'The good constables of Strathclyde can on occasion behave a trifle peculiarly but they generally don't just snatch random members of the public and have them charged with major crimes. They usually have a reason,

Alan. Now, how did they know you were visiting her that afternoon?'

'Say they've witnesses who saw me leave her flat. Well, leave the building anyway. Must be nosey parker neighbours. When I was over in the pub I was talking to a couple of old boys who knew her. Talking about Red Clydeside and the like. John Maclean. Keir Hardie. The old days when they thought a Scottish workers republic was a possibility. I imagine I got pretty pissed. Can still feel the bevvy. Keep thinking I'm going to wake up any minute. Know the feeling?'

'Vaguely.' Taking notes with nearly unsteady hands.

'And would you believe one of the coppers from here actually saw me standing out there on the pavement and saw Debs pull up in the van and me bawl her out?' He sighed and shook his head. 'Any road what kind of sick-o kills old women? I mean you'd have to be fairly brain damaged to be into that. Agreed? Some whacked out looney. Well, that sticks me in it. Right? Up to the neck. Right? 'Cause just how's anybody going to find him? The one as really did kill her? I mean they've got me so nobody's looking any more. Are they? Got another cigarette?'

'Mr Naylor?' What was wrong? Had she difficulty recognising him?

Naylor peered at her and she peered back. Even in the dim light of her cell she looked like no-one so much as Muriel Grey, Naylor's all time-and-space favourite TV presenter, with the crop of yellow hair and the angular nipped face and small full lipped mouth. She also had the same sensational legs. At five foot ten in her stocking soles she was taller but the main difference between her and

Munchable Muriel was the voice. Terribly well enunciated. The kind of pronunciation frightfully well received in all the correct restaurants and at every weekend's huntin-shootin-fishin.'

'You okay Debs?' Door whumped shut behind and the key clickclacked in the lock.

'Oh, thank God you're here. Thank God. I thought I was dreaming when you came through that door. They think I've killed Lexie Beattie. Killed her!'

She had crushed herself up in the corner like a discarded ball of paper, arms tight around the folded legs, face pressed onto the knees showing through the splits in the bluejeans. Was this fashion or poverty? She's an Oxford graduate. Enough money in the bank to holiday in Kenya last year. Must be fashion? And shivering in her black biker's jacket even though the heating's full on.

'I know, Debs. The press are nosing about outside something ferocious.'

'What did you say to them? You didn't mention me did you? My father'll just die! Have you seen Alan yet? How is he? Is he all right?'

'Yes, he's fine. Up to high doh but keeping a lid on it.'

'Have the pigs beaten him up or anything?' There was a catch in her breath.

'Look who in their right mind's going to try beating up Banksie? Never insult a corporation bus. D'you follow me?'

'I just thought … well, y'know, there's so many stories …'

'Forget them. What have the police asked you about all this?'

'Nearly three hours of questioning. I didn't realise

how exhausting it can be. I could sleep for a week.'

'Did you tell them about the character in Asda?'
'I told them everything I could recall. They looked rather dubious.'

'About this character you picked up in Asda; it's impor— '

'Picked up? I beg you pardon! I do not go round shopping for men at Asda, Mr Naylor! If you must know – '

'No, no. Let me rephrase that …'

'– this particular man stopped me just beyond the checkout and said he wondered if I was with the peace camp van. It was in the car park and its pretty difficult to miss and I always wear my peace button and my badges. So he stopped me. Very polite and civil he was too. He expressed a very keen interest. Asked about joining. What was involved. What he'd be expected to do. I said okay he – '

'I get the picture. I'm sorry. I'm sorry …'

' – could at least come and talk it over with Alan so long as he understood that there was no way I could personally guarantee he would be accepted into the group. I asked what he knew of the problems associated with Glen Douglas – '

'Shut up! That's enough!'

'There's no need to be rude, Mister Naylor.'

'We need that guy as a witness. So between now and when I come back here to see you this afternoon which'll be around threeish you put your brain onto piecework and dig up everything you can remember about him. Everything. Was he tall short fat skinny? Colour of his eyes. His hair? Long short spiked streaked? Clothes. Denims? Cords? What badges? What kind of shoes? What kind of accent? Did he limp? Was he a hunchback? Got the picture? Right?'

She started to cry. Naylor left feeling nasty and twisted. One might conceivably have handled that with a trifle more diplomacy? Blame the hangover.

The reporters in the foyer had been flagged that the defence solicitor in their prize murder case had arrived but he was quick. Nobody knew him. Unrecognised he could be CID or some other lawyer. 'Hey! You! Are you John Naylor?' one shouted. Naylor chilled up a sneer and torpedoed through them.

'Well well well, stone the proverbial crows,' Naylor said to the figure descending the stairs towards him. 'The redoubtable Detective Sergeant "Flan the Man" Flanagan in person, no less.' He held out his hand and the policeman took it, face breaking into a wide smile. Back in the days when Flanagan had been busting peace campers and Naylor was springing them Flanagan's placid style and supercool dress sense was the envy of the lawyer's green little heart.

Today was no different. Hair centre parted with big bushy waves, gold rim half moon specs, long Italian tan coat and the fifty quid baseball trainers. And always the laid back poise.

'Hey, good to see you, Jack. But, er, wait for it ... Detective Inspector now.'

'Tut tut, vaulting ambition o'er leaping itself and all that?'

The policeman shrugged, 'The years passed by but promotion didn't. Should've realised you'd be in on this though. Still cleaning the campers' noses?'

'Absolutely.'

'How are they? How're Susan and Donnie and the babies?'

'Well the babies are at nursery now. In fact the oldest's going into primary about now, I think. So what're you doing here?'

'Well, really I ought to be flying my desk back at Pitt Street but this mess happening at the weekend, and Cranstonhill's a wee shop, well, all sorts of oddities like me are turning up. Listen, Jack I'm a bit pinched for time. You go on up. Tell the constable on the door I sent you. And, em, I'll tell you what. We'll meet beginning of next week. I'll give you a rundown. Okay? Wee pint and a blether? Fancy?'

'Know me, Flan. Refuse nothing but blows.'

'Monday Tuesday then. Oh, listen there's a DS Rose in the flat. Tell him to put a jildy on, will you? I can't hang about all day.'

The smell in the close was familiar and unwelcome, cats' piss and stale cabbage. Naylor detested it. He waltzed briefly with the young constable on the landing outside Lexie Beattie's flat. The baby plod kept stepping aside into the lawyer's path. Eventually, blushing, he just stood still and let Naylor walk muttering round him to the open storm doors.

Make it at least look like you know what you're about, Naylor told himself. He examined the storm doors. Thick and heavy but well oiled. One of those little peepholes, two safety chains and a big newish looking bolt. Then he turned to the inner front door, mahogany with a glossy veneer and a big stained glass panel with a few sections in simple frosted glass beside the Yale lock. Naylor nodded sagely, that is to say carefully, remembering that the

37

brain was capable of independent motion within his skull until all alcohol left his bloodstream.

Who was he trying to impress? Baby plod didn't care: he was too busy trying to look the part of a grown up fully feathered policeman. There was a smell, something recently burned. Sniffing, Naylor walked into the lobby almost tripping over the uplifted carpet and the loosened floorboards. What's all this, then? He looked about meticulously counting four doors, bedroom, lounge, kitchen ...

And a bathroom.

A long very narrow old fashioned bathroom with an old fashioned cast iron bath on wee squat legs, big brass taps on both it and the chunky white handbasin, again old fashioned, and an old fashioned bog with the cistern up against the ceiling and a detective atop a rickety ladder right beside it. To be accuarte, a red haired white faced detective in chocolate leatherette bumfreezer and thick black cords perched on top, sleeve rolled up, arm in cistern ... He looked at Naylor, stopped still and his face reset like a TV abruptly switched to a blank channel.

'Who the fuck're you!'

A man with style caught in the act. In what act Naylor could not figure just yet. But whatever, Naylor had caught him.

'John Naylor, Munro Kerr Meikle, agents for the accused. Inspection of locus. With the permission of DI Flanagan. And you, sir, are Detective Sergeant Rose? DI Flanagan entreats you to join him downstairs.'

Dropping a towel as he reached the floor he said, 'Good morning'. Never once looking at Naylor, just straightening, smoothing his sleeve and manoeuvring out into he lobby and through the front door.

Naylor asked 'By the way what's the significance of the cistern?' No reply.

The detective's heels echoed in the stairwell. Naylor said to the young constable, 'Who're they?'

He shrugged, 'Pitt Street. Who knows? They're new to me.'

'Pitt Street? How come Regional Police Headquarters are involved. When'd they turn up?'

'Were here when I arrived, sir. That was just over an hour ago.'

'Flanagan and Rose? Sound like a couple of comic singers.'

'Pardon, sir?'

Naylor pulled back the lounge curtain in time to see a big black Citroen swing away from the kerb and roll off towards St Vincent Street. Interesting. What kind of cop would use a Citroen, a car not easily made as a police car? Drug Squad? Task Force?

Special Branch ...

The lounge itself was a curious mixture of design. For sitting down there was a fairly new, fairly cheap moss green three piece suite, light and functional and expertly shredded, chunks of bright beige foam scattered across the floor. Against the wall, two upright glass-fronted bookcases, possibly Victorian, both open and empty. Their contents piled in several untidy heaps on a very large, very solid old oak table. In the large alcove originally intended to hold a recessed boxed-in bed stood a midi hi-fi unit. The records and compact discs were also heaped naked on the table, the sleeves and cases, some torn some broken, were scattered around the table on the floorboards. He noticed maybe four or five dozen empty cassette cases. But no tapes on the table. No tapes anywhere. The carpet had been rolled back. He unrolled it a little and put on the critical eye. A powder blue Persian. Very nice. Go well in a Young Executive Studio Flat. Hmmm.

The walls had been crowded with framed photographs and there were still maybe thirty in place with half as many missing. Floral wallpaper glowed from the vacant oblong and oval lots.

There were sepias of long ago family and friends mixed in with crisp black and whites and even colour pics from the last twenty years. Lexie with Jim Sillars at a Scottish Labour Party conference. With Robin Cook and Anna McCurley on a BBC Question Time. Sitting on an overstuffed sofa with Wendy Wood. Embracing a grinning Gordon Wilson at some election victory. Marching beside Bruce Kent. Drinking with Bertrand Russell. Here she was, middle aged, with Bevan. There she was, a young woman, with George Bernard Shaw.

Naylor turned to the books. Mostly political material. Mostly socialist. Marx and Engels. He rummaged past it looking for something different. My God, *Mein Kampf!* Then social history. Smout. Numerous volumes from the Left Wing Book Club yellowed with the decades. Biographies. Lenin. Keir Hardie. John Maclean. James Maxton. Some CND pamphlets. Spaven's *Fortress Scotland*. Bunyard's *Nuclear Britain*. A copy of *Unlikely Stories, Mostly* by Alasdair Gray with a personalised dedication running in a square around the title page. MacDiarmid's *Complete Poems* signed 'To our White Rose.'

There was a writing desk in one corner by the

window. Only a scatter of notepaper. No letters. Not a document in sight, letter, receipt, nothing. The two drawer filing cabinet beside it was missing both drawers.

Bastards cleaned the place out!

The bedroom was sad. They'd torn open the mattress and gutted the wardrobe. Some old jackets and coats lying razor-worked in strips on the floorboards. But the kitchen was worst by far. The contents of every container had been dumped, some in the sink, some on the table, most on the floor. Brown rice, pasta, semolina, Fruit 'n Fibre, flour, sugar, Flash, golden breadcrumbs, oatmeal, and that was only what he could identify, and it was everywhere. All the fitted kitchen cupboard space had been cleared. Pots, pans, saucepans lay tossed in a heap in one corner. Cups, mugs, glassware, plates, sideplates, bowls all lay stacked on the table partly covered by the mess. And brown smears in the sink; somebody burned papers and mashed the ash in water.

'Jee-zuz ...'

More floorboards were up. What were they looking for? Her two kilos of coke? Her atom bomb plans? And who did the looking, Flanagan and Rose? Or the killer?

Would it not have been terribly useful to take some nice polaroids right now? Camera purchased, as a matter of interest, with a view to situations just like this. Always kept in the boot which seemed like a good idea. But where is the car right now? Who knows? The Dumbuck? The Maltings? The Mato Grosso?

Ouch! Don't think of the Maltings!

The kitchen window looked out over a high barbed-wire wall to Argyle Street: an orange double-decker bombed past lights still on even in the bright morning.

Naylor nodded, driver was probably running late. Then he examined the white marks on the floor. A distorted oblong with feet. This was where they found her. Lying by the sink in a coma. Battered stupid according to the Cranstonhill cops. Died in the Western intensive care unit just over an hour later. Should've died in her bed, surrounded by her family and friends and her memories. Poor old soul. Naylor felt a knot start in his throat, tears rimming the eyes.

What's this! Get a grip, Jack!

He sniffed hard. He double swallowed and cleared his throat.

Don't get dragged in. Never get personally involved: cardinal rule for every practising criminal lawyer from Dar-es-Salaam to Dennistoun. First murder you've touched, probably the biggest criminal trial you'll ever handle and you lose muscle tone right at the start. Come on, man. You're going to have to lay off the hard stuff if it does this to old the professional composure!

The young policeman was dreamy eyed; his face said he was miles away. Naylor stood between the front door and the storm doors looking at him for a moment. Then he spoke. 'Who made the mess in there?'

'Oh, er …Sorry, sir. Emm..' The final answer was a shrug. 'I've no' been inside yet myself, sir. But there were a lot of people going through the place when I turned up. You'd really have to get in touch with Cranstonhill. Maybe Pitt Street.'

'Maybe right enough. If you're fed up read one of those books in there. A wee bit of enlightenment, you know.' A dangerous thing, he added mentally. And smiled and went down the stairs.

The Boulevard car honked twice and pulled up.

Harry was at the wheel. Naylor smiled, his luck was changing. He came out the close and there they were. The Newshounds. And this time they were ready for him.

There were maybe a dozen, fifteen of them. Who was he? Was he representing both Banks and Mooney? What did he think of it? And where did he come from?

'Atlantis.'

'Eh?'

'A wee joke.'

So he gave them his name, clearly, mentioned the firm and made sure they had a few nice head and shoulders shots with the chin up so the thinning hair was less obvious. Agent for the accused he told them raising their eyebrows, drawing a few frowns. Who is this geezer? Is he really handling a murder trial this size? Him? Not Beltrami? Not Bob MacCormack or Andrew Gallen?

Man of mystery. Dark Horse.

Naylor loved it!

Three:Moderato

SLEEP, SLEEP, SLEEP. Absolutely definitely utterly must get the head down.

As he scaled the flights to his flat he could hear the 'phone shrieking on the wall. Cursing he let himself in and lifted the handset and grunted into it.

'Mister, you Banks' brief then?' It was a very very Glaswegian voice.

'Who wants to know?'

'Umm.' There was a small sigh. 'Name's Haggerty. It's this thing about Lexie Beattie. Y'know, pal, this woman that was killed.'

He pronounced it 'kilt.'

'The murder? What about it? Listen, where d'you get my name and my phone number?'

'Heeeeey, keep the heid. Y'were on Radio Clyde and you're in the phone book. Okay? Right? Well, er, look ... I might want to talk to you, pal.'

'Might? What d'you mean might? If you've anything, any kind of information bearing on this case then come forward. People are facing life sentences here. Pal!'

'Mmmm, er ... Well. Naw, I've got to get you

45

checked out first.'

'What? Checked out?'

'Aye. Y'know what I mean ... Wee bit of the positive vetting. Okay? Right? No big deal, pal. If you're clean I'll be in the Turkish Café in High Street at one on Sunday, tomorrow. Back booth. You can buy me my dinner. Stay cool 'n that.' Clickrrrrr ...

Naylor glared through the pale grey plaster ceiling out into the cosmos beyond. 'Loonies and wankers, that's all I totally don't need, God! Thanks a billion, God!' He dropped the receiver and fell face down on the bed.

For the second time that day the phone woke him after less than four hours sleep. This time he surfaced to a world of dry pain.

He let the machine ring and made for the toilet and stuck his head under the shower face up, opened his mouth and let the cold water hit him. The old phone just went on clawing at the wall so he knew it was the police. People only have that much patience if they're paid for it.

'What's up now? I don't believe this, it's not even noon yet.'

'Mr Naylor? This is Constable Carmichael at Cranstonhill, sir. Sorry to disturb you again. Just to let you know that charges against Deborah Mooney are being dropped and she'll be released within the hour.'

'Uh. Right.'

In the back of Harry's car, in the process of being beamed up to the Dumbuck Hotel, Naylor realised that Debs Mooney looked passably acceptable. Even in the split knee jeans. Even in the less than normally charitable light of day. Then he frowned. She's still shivering. What is this? Does shock last this long? Is she on something, coming down?

'It was the check-out girl at Asda. She remembered me going through. It was all the peace badges and CND stickers on the jacket. And she saw this chap I met there, the one who wanted to join us. She thought he looked like he might be a mugger or a rapist or something of that order. And it happened just before she took her break so she knew the time. She also mentioned it to a few of her friends during the break. Apparently she came forward this morning. Oh God bless her.'

'It's all over the front of the papers, all over the radio and tele. You're national news, Debs. Well, the killing is anyway.'

'Not the best publicity we might have hoped for.' Lower lip pouting and trembling.

Jackie, there is definitely a little-girl-lost performance in progress here. What we must determine is whether it is natural or a put on. No simple task with the Naylor mouth tasting like an open wound going gangrenous. The entire head and contents going gangrenous. Can she see it? Why should you worry? Well? You're not trying to get off with her or anything. Are you? Well? Are you?

Come on! We do not mess about with the clients! Are we going brain dead or what?

From a detached viewpoint he could agree that she was quite pretty. She had the longest shapeliest legs he had ever been this close to, a considerable factor for a leg man like himself. Trouble only came in maintaining this detached viewpoint. What was wrong? Where did this mob of gross hormones spring from? Could she tell he was less than optimum right now? Did he smell? Even after the shower? Perhaps he might pull over, drop casually into a chemist and hare about buying up an armful of stick deodorants, Amplex, Durex?

Stop thinking like this!

Anyway she probably sees it differently. Probably sees Jackie Naylor as a vulnerable chap; maybe well bred women like her could glimpse the delicate soul beneath the crisp pro carapace? The nineties (or was it the eighties) man? No?

This was one of Naylor's favourite fantasies, one of his Linus blankets. He loved to imagine his true value, his depths, had never been properly appreciated. He knew that his wife, during their brief but loud marriage, had never once laid eyes on what he regarded as his essential self. After all, was not this the man who loved Dvorak? And not just the New World Symphony either, the Serenade for Strings, Romance, the cello and violin concertos? Was not this the man who had actually read and almost understood every word of Hofstadter's *Godel, Escher and Bach*? Who also had a modest, although he liked to think impressive, collection of works on the Impressionists? And there were three books, the ones on Manet, Cézanne and Degas that were particular humdingers.

Surely this had to be a man of some grace, some sensitivity? The kind of man who would in other circumstances be found of an early Sunday morning reading the review supplements, glass of Buck's Fizz to hand, munching hot lightly buttered oatcakes while listening to a Radio Three concert?

He nibbled his lower lip and wondered and covertly eyed her legs and listened to not one word she uttered.

By the time they reached the Dumbuck she'd been wittering on about hang-gliding for almost ten minutes.

Naylor was making sage echoing noises, nodding. Praying that all would be well. He almost wept when he saw the Nova. It was pristine, untouched, beautiful. And he'd been smart enough to keep the soft top in place so the interior was dry, warm even. The keys were still in the the jacket he'd left in the hotel. Luck was with him here too, his Visa and Access cards sat still snug and safe in their little credit card pocket.

Just at the instant his trepidation transformed to delight he glanced at Debs Mooney and caught a fleeting indefinable expression on her face. What was it? Had the hangover become visible? Was his pain leeching pity from her? Or was it the sudden smile, his boyishness and charm sunbursting through the gloom? Had he known more women he might have recognised it as a brief signature of that disappointment, probably genetic in nature, they all eventually discover for men.

He favoured her with an extra boyish grin as he opened the car door. Cocked his head to one side. Very nearly cheeky. 'Permission to come aboard, ma'am.'

She made a brief nervous smile and climbed in. He closed the door and started rounding the car. As he did so hideous misshapen memories lurched from the suddenly gothic proportions of the Dumbuck. Quickly he packed himself behind the wheel and pulled out of the car park, turning right and heading westerly smartish. But not too smart.

He picked up the white Ford Sierra in the rear view mirror before he was clear of Dumbarton. To be positive he did a few fancy turns now up this street then down that one. They were tailing him.

Stay with it. Keep the head. Drive nicely. Nobody's

going to do anything if you're a good boy. But why were they there? What kind of deep shit was he getting into?

Or was he in it already?

Well, there was the deep shit with Melanie Forbes. Another shipwrecked relationship. You really set yourself up for these, Jackie. It's unbelievable how totally predictable you've become. It takes maybe three, four months to shape yourself as a nice funny caring character; someone not too heavy, just sufficiently exposed. Then when it looks as near perfect as its ever going to be you pitch a bowling ball at it. Ka-Pow! Crash clatter tinkle ...

And now you're entertaining thoughts sweet and salacious about the woman on your left. By the way, why has she gone quiet all of a sudden? Has she made the Strathclyde Police standard issue unmarked vehicle? Still hanging on, three cars back now. If all the field manuals and spy thrillers were right they'd spell it with another car. Or maybe not. Maybe they thought he wouldn't suspect. That was their trouble, no concept of habit formed from paranoia.

All those years with Army Intelligence in Berlin and West Germany chewed up one's behaviour patterns.

Read my file, boys.

'You've gone helluva quiet on me, Debs? Problems?'

'No. I'm just thinking about yesterday, about last night.'

Thank you for mentioning last night.

What had he done? Exactly what happened, actual events, details? Naylor tried thinking cold and hard. No use; his memories were all rotted cheesecloth, full of holes, came apart as he fingered them. But what little was there stirred nausea in his guts and he pulled the car round a corner at Cardross and got out at the railway station.

'I need some air. I'll be back in a wee minute.'

He sat on the beach, stared into the distance until the feeling passed. Across a couple of miles of river Port Glasgow looked wonderful. Like most places in Naylor's life it lost its magic on closer examination but from here it was just fine. She sat down beside him and asked what was wrong and he told her it had nothing to do with the case or her. Things were a bit messy in his private life and now and then it got to him. Did she understand? She nodded. He wondered if she was tempted to comfort him. Certainly he would be tempted to accept any comforts on offer. It was symptomatic of a problem which had fettered him since adolescence; he always waited for the woman to make the first move. Not out of coyness. More like the good gun-fighter at the big showdown just as the picture's climaxing, facing the baddie in the street with his hand hovering over the gunbutt waiting for him to make that one move which would let everyone in the audience know it was now morally a hundred percent okay for the goodie to blow him to bits ... He frowned at the odious craving for moral superiority, at the bizarre comparison: women and bad-guy gunfighters? Something Freudian in that.

After a couple of minutes' awkwardly growing silence they returned to the car.

The post-bevvy munchies had him. Even thinking about thinking about food flooded his mouth with saliva. The prospect of lunch at Paul Goldman's had been luring him along the coast road and almost kept him going. Almost. Paul was definitely one of the best but maybe he could be a bit stuffy if one brought an uninvited guest to lunch. Like one's client, just out of pokey with the murder charge scarcely gone cold on her. Naylor whinged and dragged himself up the A832 at Helensburgh. Promised himself the best food the Inverbeg Inn could conjure this afternoon and made for the peace camp.

After a while she said, 'It really is terribly nice of you to drive me out here. I appreciate it. I do, you know.'

'Uh? Oh, s'alright. Hardly leave you to walk it.' He smiled his plain brand X smile. She smiled back and this took him by surprise.

'I ... didn't realise you had personal problems. One doesn't really think of one's doctor or lawyer having problems, if you see what I mean. Well at least not when one's in a bit of a mess as Alan and I are at the moment. I do hope none of this is making things any worse for you.'

He smiled lop-sided. 'Nothing I can't handle.' She definitely brought out the Humphrey Bogart in him. The hormone factory upped its output once more leaving him feeling good enough about himself to appreciate the scenery.

The water was choppy and grey blue. Out there were the Inches, small islands topped with trees, the occasional one with a house. The far shore sloped away to mountains, up to the massif that started with Ben Lomond at the head of the loch and ran all the way to the coastlines facing the Western Isles, the last realms of Gaeldom. Naylor sighed. A shiver of Celtic Twilight rippled through him. The splendour, the grandeur, the majesty.

And then the peace camp.

It festered garish and grubby on the lochside facing the entrance to Glen Douglas. Faded yellow lettering on a tired banner proclaimed its identity. Three caravans adorned with peace symbols and slogans and washing strung on lines between them. Half a dozen placards propped up at the road's edge. NATO'S NUCLEAR KITCHEN and BEAUTY & THE BOMB and ALL THIS & APOCALYPSE TOO and TAKE THE HIGH ROAD – TO ARMAGEDDON, the latter with an arrow pointing up the glen.

'I'm going to eat. Want to join me?'

'Er … Thanks but no. I must tell the others about everything.'

'Right. I'll be back down here in about an hour,' he said as he pulled up. She jumped from the car and trotted to the largest of the caravans. There were faces at the window. The door was opening.

Naylor shouted, 'And don't forget to pack a bag for him.'

As he was leaving the car park facing the hotel he was almost run over by a white Sierra turning in. He vickied the driver. The driver did nothing nor did the man beside him and when the car came to a halt they just sat there. Naylor swallowed back his rage and crossed the road and went straight into the dining room. He took a window seat and looked out but you couldn't see the Sierra from his position and he hadn't had a good enough look at the occupants to ID them.

Sigh sigh sigh. Never let paranoia stand in the way of a good lunch. He ordered the veal and declined the wine list in favour of Highland Spring.

What was going to come of last night? By Monday it should be the talk of the steamie. The Partners will certainly have heard. He'd be in St Vincent Place explaining it away. Nicely. My granny died and I was a trifle over-wrought? My girlfriend gave me the push? Sound like excuses for dogging school. I was on medication and the drink must've overreacted with it? Or what about the truth? I was set up by that bastard Lambie. Sipping his white wine fucking spritzers and loading me up with Absolut trebles. So I could be the prime entertainment at his exclusive little engagement party! He'd never have sprung it on me if I hadn't already belted back a few after a totally shitty Friday.

Language, John. Language.

Jee-zuz, sitting right here looking at the waiter approaching to take his order Naylor could hear Big Bill Nicholson's words rolling in through his left ear. Nicholson, a man deeply affected by the timbre of his own voice, trained it for amateur opera, modelled it on Burton. Legend had it he was considering a career at the Bar when MKM made their offer of a junior partnership back in the early sixties. The Bar would have better suited his talents for melodrama and the Grand Gesture. Still as a senior partner he now had more scope for theatricals.

Remember his very first words at the interview?

'John Daniel Naylor. It certainly has a decided poetic ring to it. But I believe they call you "Jack"?'

Naylor knew the score before he laid eyes on MKM or Big Bill. The MoD had been specific. They would fix it for him to leave the Army, go on the Reserve List and find a plum little position in civvy street. In return he would use same plum little position, in MKM's Dumbarton office, to afford them some small assistance in his known area of expertise – intelligence.

They would like him to gain the confidence of the Glen Douglas peace campers, eventually represent them in all matters. Chat them up. Make them relax. Encourage them to talk and talk and talk. And send in monthly reports to Kentigern House. And if anything critical arose, inform

W.K. Nicholson.

Well, a murder should be critical enough. Better call Big Bill after you've talked to the campers. Maximise the information content, lay it on with a road roller. Then mention last night. That's the best strategy. Give him a clear context for John William Naylor's social cum professional indiscretions. Let him deal with the rest of the Partners on Monday.

What about the Law Society? A disciplinary hearing? Nah. Bunch of old women. When was the last time they took on a partner in a big Glasgow firm? Back in the Pliocene era? They only gang up on the wee fish. There might be fireworks but nobody'll be shooting live rounds.

One hundred minutes later, replete, comfortable and confident he was strolling down to the campsite, hands in pockets. Frowning and nodding importantly. Debs Mooney came running from the largest caravan, the one which doubled as an office. Running, he decided was not her forte. Her gangling good looks went down well in repose or walking dignified and languid, which she'd probably picked up at model school or something. But not running. The long limbs positively flailed. A small leather suitcase jounced in one hand.

'This is the bag. I've packed basics, change of clothes, soap, towel, toothpaste and a couple of paperbacks.' She was breathless.

Naylor took it.

'Let's walk. I'll stick this in the boot,' he said and started strolling back towards the car park.

'Can we go inside? The others are waiting?'

'Debs, this is not a committee meeting. I want to talk to you with nobody butting in. I'm looking for information about yesterday not a brainstorming session about the best ways to take political advantage of this situation. Okay? Right? Let's go.'

'They're simply worried. That's all.'

'Good. They should be worried. This kind of publicity is just what you people don't need. Murdering an old woman. That is bad. That is almost the worst. Murdering an old woman who was also regarded with great fondness by virtually every major politico in Scotland, left and right. Well, that is the worst. If Banksie goes down for this one have you any idea what it's going to do to the peace movement? Your actual repercussions are going to hit disaster proportions throughout the UK. The popular impression of you as idealistic loonies is going to change. By Monday morning the *Sun*'ll have you branded as homicidal zealots. And if he's found guilty that's how everyone's going to see you. The national heavies. The Sundays and their colour comics. Radio. TV. The lot. You do appreciate the difference?'

'Yes. Yes, we've been talking about just that.'

'Wonderful.'

'Right. Well, we've been discussing this and I don't think you're going to be too happy about the conclusions. We feel the whole thing is an MI5 set up – '

'Jee-zuz!'

'I knew you'd be upset but – '

Naylor gave a little scream, dropped the bag and battered his fists on his head. 'What part of the bloody Solar System are you living in? I don't give a tuppeny toss about MI5 or the CIA or the KGB. The Transylvannian League of Deceased Insomniacs can be behind this for all I care. Am I communicating across these vast interplanetary distances?

I want an itemised list of every detail of every thing that has actually happened that might have some bearing on this case. Not suppositions. Not conjecture. Everything you can dredge up from that Oxford-educated memory of yours. Every. Single. Thing.'

'I know. Calm down. Calm down.' She pulled down a heavy zip on the biker jacket and took two folded A4 sheets from the pocket. 'That's what happened as I remember it. If anything else comes to mind I'll put it down and send it to you. Is it all right?'

'Hum, oh yes,' he said.

Naylor read it as they walked. He slung the bag into the Nova's boot and continued down to the lochside. They strolled by the pleasure boat jetties, waters lapping at the edge of the bank. Then they ran out of negotiable land and sat under a tree. He nodded and folded the papers, put them into his jacket. 'This is fine. It'll do for starters anyway.'

'So far as I know he has no criminal record. Will they allow bail on Monday?'

Naylor shook his head. 'Never get bail on a murder charge. Even if you're Snow White. No way.'

She lowered her head and said, 'I'm finding all this terribly difficult, you know. I really loved Lexie and I do love Alan. It's all so ... so gross, so damned ugly. And back there, back at the camp I have to be so strong, hold it all together. They depend on me and I ...'

Naylor was nodding his head. Making sympathetic sounds. Not listening. Wondering how he was going to conjure evidence up from the depths. Maybe someone at Kentigern House could run a search through a database or the like? But looking for what? Likely murderers of Lexie Beattie? No. They'd only pick up stuff on hi-tech spies and dodgy service personnel. What about the Police National Computer or MI5's Registry? Any friends that could be contacted? Any favours to call in? And then he thought, do I even want to get involved in all that anyway? What's the MoD position on the murder? On Banks being charged?

Then he realised she was crying.

Ah shit.

This was not the way it was supposed to happen. It was unfair. She hadn't comforted him when he was down. Why should he comfort her? The sobbing grew louder. Put an arm round her? Talk a load of plausible reassuring tripe? Or ignore it diplomatically? She leaned on him, pressed her head on his shoulder. Well, that tore it. Naylor grimaced and, looking about furtively, patted the short blond hair. No, she wasn't his type after all. No, really. Too gaunt, looked too much like David Bowie. That's enough patting the hair. Pat the hand now and grip it and hold it quite firmly. But what d'you actually say to her? Actually put into words and phrases? Chin up, old thing? Pip pip? What would you have said back in the army?

He gripped her by the waist and stood and said, 'Let's walk back a bit.'

She threw her arms round him and wept louder. Now her whole body leaded in against him. Naylor felt the first hot lick of lust in his groin and didn't like it. Reminded him too much of the disastrous marriage he'd packed away with other attic memories of his earlier life. And there was the panic that ensued when real life intruded on his private universe of sex fantasy.

Still, she a kind of gamine charm ... No, that's just the hormone factory talking.

He tried walking. 'This is not getting us anywhere,

Debs. Come on now. Get a grip.' But she limpeted along, arms still round him, sobs still shaking her bony frame.

'I can't. Just can't.' And so saying she sank to a crouch still bubbling and snorting. He dug in his pockets for a handkerchief but it was more show than substance; he knew he didn't have one, never carried them. At least she wasn't clinging to him any more. He grabbed her under one shoulder and helped her up, surprised at how light she was for so tall a woman. Maybe she was anorexic? The thought of sex with a Belsen victim lacked a certain beauty, dignity, blemished one's self-image. He felt the last of the lust flicker out.

He firmly disentangled her and started walking along a jetty which protruded out into the loch. Large cabin cruisers lay tied up alongside. She trotted behind.

There was a landing stage at the jetty's end. Naylor gripped the rail and stared resolutely across at Rowardennan.

'How many are living in the camp just now?'

'Five of us and the three children. Four with Alan in custody.'

'Not a lot. Is it?'

'We're always talking about abandoning it and going across to the Faslane camp but then we'll have some big event and it keeps us going.'

'How did Alan get on with Lexie Beattie?'

She sighed, looked pained. She leaned back against the rail and folded her arms, frowned at Naylor, her eyes still red, cheeks still flushed from crying. 'Why do you ask?'

'I want to know what you told the police. That's why.'

'I told them that she doted on him.'

'Which is, I assume, a lie.'

'Oh, I suppose they got on well enough. Lexie was an anglophobe. She only tolerated Alan because he was working class and his parents were second generation Irish.'

'So where did that leave her and you?'

'My father's Irish, my mother's Welsh and I was born in Canada. Satisfied?'

'So you lied to the police to protect him?'

She shrugged. 'Suppose so.'

'You realise the truth will come out in court? It will make things look so much worse for him? It will emphasise to the jury that you, his lover, feel you have to lie to save his skin.' She said nothing but her chin sank to her chest. For a panicky moment he thought she was going to erupt with tears again.

'What else did you lie about?'

She shook her head. 'Nothing.'

'Nothing. All right. What was it you left out? Didn't tell them?'

She sucked her lower lip for a moment. 'Alan was a captain in the paras.'

'The paras? The Parachute Regiment? Shitabrick. How many people know that?'

'He was actually recruited by me, if that's the right expression. He came by here on a hiking holiday in Easter 1988. He was quite interested. He said right away that he was newly out of the Army. Never made a secret of it. And, well, people with military knowledge are really valuable so we invited him to stay. He said he'd think it over and went off on his hiking holiday. Came back a month later and has been here ever since. Everyone at the camp knows.'

'Did Lexie Beattie know?'

'Obviously,' she said quickly.

It was Naylor's turn to sigh and drop his chin, look down at the water and see image of himself looking back, apparently as far below the surface as he was above it.

'Alright. What else?'

'She ... It must have been a chance in a million. She knew someone who served under him a few years ago. Said Alan was a complete fascist.'

Boy oh boy, Jackie. This gets better all the time. He shook his head. 'What's this character's name?'

'I'm not sure. Hannah or Hanley or something like that.'

'Not ... Haggerty?' The name of the looney who was going to have Naylor "vetted" before he'd say anything to him.

Her voice was smaller, shallower. 'I think so. Neither of us met him. She only mentioned him on Tuesday last.'

'Okay, I understand Alan was trying to gain her support for some kind of big event?'

'He has a plan for a kind of national observing network which should determine the route of materials coming into the Glen.' As she spoke she grew more animated, more aggressive. Naylor watched, fascinated. 'That way we will establish that there is a direct link between the nuclear warhead production facilities and here. The government and NATO both claim there are no connections. If we can establish that there clearly is a connection, that the Glen is in fact one of the largest nuclear weapons stores in Europe we'll embarrass the hell out of them on television and in the press. We'll give the peace movement more credibility and impetus than its had since Cruise came to Britain!'

He started back down the jetty and she followed, still talking, gesticulating.

She said, 'That's what I was going to tell you when you arrived and it really is important. We think its MI5 setting him up. They've certainly got wind of what we're up to by now. We think they killed her and framed Alan for it. I'm sure that's what's happened.'

'Not a chance,' Naylor said. The words were out before he could pull them back so he continued. 'Er … MI5 and such organisations may well set people up on occasion, people they see as dangerous, but I understand they don't tend to use murder as the means of putting their targets, er, victims away.'

'Why not?'

'They prefer setting people up for armed robbery if at all possible. You see it's unlikely that someone going down for murder will be in prison for more than five years. With a half decent armed robbery, on the other hand, you can count on twice maybe three times that.'

She shook her head. 'Impossible. They'd never find Alan anywhere near a bank. No, it's definitely MI5.' She smiled knowingly at him. 'Oh, I know you think it's not but just wait and see.'

'Hmph. Good idea.'

They had reached the Nova. He opened the door. She threw her arms about him and kissed him hard on the mouth. He did not pull away, just stuck his brain onto record for replaying later.

She said, 'Thanks for talking to me. I feel so much more together now and I know you'll do your absolute best for Alan!'

He nodded. 'Absolutely. Er ... maybe you'd like some dinner ... later. I could call by maybe sevenish?'

She looked startled. 'Well ... that should be very nice.'

What the hell are you doing, Jackie? Are you having a breakdown or something? Dinner with a client? A client whose beloved is up on a murder charge? Bewildered at his own behaviour, Naylor climbed into the Nova and executed a smart three point turn. She waved and he quickly returned it and accelerated back towards Glasgow. He didn't even give the white Sierra a glance in passing. Two men stood in the hotel doorway, one holding his zoom lensed camera on Naylor, finishing off the roll of pictures.

Rrikikikikik ...

Four:Staccato

'SOCIALISING WITH THE clients is one thing if you're a fiscal and the clients are the police, old chum, or maybe you're into company law and you're trying to win over a big corporation for your firm. But – and its a big But – when you're doing criminal work – which you are – it is not advisable to have dinner with your latest case.'

Paul Goldman gave Naylor his startled and haunted look. It was as if he was seeing something surprisingly ghastly in the depths of his friend's soul. He usually switched it on last thing on Blitz Night when Naylor would suggest they were sober enough to drive home.

Naylor smirked and said, 'Crap.'

They were in the narrow kitchen at the back of Goldman's house in Rhu. Goldman referred to it as "the Cottage". That was how it had been advertised in the *Glasgow Herald* property pages. A seven room, two loo residence with conservatory, a front lawn the size of a professional tennis court and a back garden big enough for a nine hole golf course. And all Goldman ever played was poker.

'Not crap. Fact, old chum.' When he said "Old

chum" he generally pushed the bridge of his gold rim glasses aggressively up his nose. 'I personally almost passed out when you told me who she was. I nearly slid to the floor. Can you believe that?'

Naylor kept smirking, 'No.'

'She,' prodding his finger in the direction of the doorway, 'is an exercise in trouble. You've never done anything like this before. What's happened? Are you cracking up? I'm serious.'

'This has upset your plans. Paul. Here you were trying to matchmake me with your sister and –' Naylor snapped his fingers and shook his head, '– don't I go dropping wrenches into the works.'

'Not at all, Jackie. Seriously. I'm just disappointed that you would bring a woman involved in a notorious murder case into my house. Especially one of those butter-wouldn't-melt-in-my-mouth kind of women. All eyes and legs and Oh so sweet and innocent by the way. Huh.'

Naylor leered. 'You really fancy her, don't you?'

'Fancy her? Fancy her? Are you joking?'

'Ho. Ho.'

'Christ, pull that disgusting expression off your face, Naylor'

'Uhuh. You can't say that. Rules of the game, sorry.'

'Can't say what?'

'Can't say "Christ". You're Jewish. It sounds ridiculous.'

'Try and be serious. Just for thirty seconds.'

'Judaism is a serious business. You've always said so and you're the only Hymie I know. Let's face it. You could not care less about her. The only bee in your bunnet is the Nazi Holocaust. And that particular bee's the size of a bus by the way.'

Paul smiled. 'Okay. Okay you want to play it like that. So you want to change the subject. Fine. You had a splendid little old time to yourself last night did you? Want to tell me about it? All the fun and games in the Maltings function suite?'

Naylor sagged. 'Oh shite. Who told you?'

'Piccolo mondo, dear friend, and a particularly small world where we ex-fiscals are concerned.'

'Oh it was dire. Dire. I keep running it over in my mind. And I imagine myself up in front of the Law Society. You know – conduct unbecoming and murmuring a judge, all that rubbish ... '

Paul's frown degenerated into an evil grin. 'Wish I'd seen it. Mind you the Law Society won't come near you. You'll raise a few smiles when you walk into court for the next ten, twenty years but nothing more.'

Ruth Goldman said, 'What's this, then? Abandoning us to each other and hoarding your many charms?' as she walked in arms laden with dishes. 'Good. Wash these and bring through some coffee.' The plates clattered onto the work surface. She wiped her hands on a dishcloth and turned for the door. A petite brunette, once very pretty, she was now more fat than plump.

'You ladies aren't tearing each others eyes out yet, then?' Paul smiled a moulded plastic smile. 'Hmmmmm?'

'Not yet. Deborah does seem rather limited in her range though. If you follow me.'

Naylor groaned quietly. Paul's wife barely approved of him. As her family lived in Basingstoke and Paul's consisted of a mother in a nursing home and a solitary married sister, Naylor was marginally useful as a babysitter for the twin seven year old daughters. The kids once thought Naylor was wonderful. His concept of babysitting was to bring along an bagful of the latest kiddy videos from Azad (his bottle of Absolut hidden discreetly under a black pudding supper at the bottom of the bag). With a good feed inside him he could get quietly, agreeably tanked without showing it. Of late however the girls were showing signs of echoing their mother's distant disapproval.

He said, 'Is she going on about the murder?'

Ruth gave him a blank look. She said, 'She's talking about the armed forces, Jack, their nuclear weapons and their oppression of the last vestige of the British Empire which apparently is Northern Ireland. Fascinating. Irene is riveted.' And she walked out.

Paul and his sister Irene looked so alike Naylor kept seeing her as Paul in drag.

Naylor puckered his lips briefly. 'I think your wife yearns secretly for my body. This veneer of contempt is how she's trying to deal with it.'

Paul shrugged. 'Stranger things,' he said.

'But not many, eh?' Naylor added. Paul glanced at him and poured coffee from the machine's big glass jug into a pot.

'Too true, not many. And I'll tell you something else for nothing, old pal. Irene's quite right about Deborah. She's weird into the bargain.'

Debs' idea of dressing for dinner was jeans without holes in the knees and a matching denim shirt with no biker's jacket. She still wore the same battered trainers. He placed a silver tray on the glass topped coffee table in front of her. There was the slender gleaming pot from which wafted the perfume of Paul's Brazil/Kenya mix. Beside it were five exquisite little cups, spoons in the saucers, a bowl of muscovado and a plate of crisp chocolate mint wafers. None of this elegance penetrated Debs' remote universe.

She turned to him and said, 'Irene tells me you were in the Army?' There was no accusation in the tone, just a querulousness. Debs was peeved.

'I've never made a secret of it,' he lied, sitting back on the canvas covered sofa, raising the eyebrows and looking at Paul. 'Have I?'

'Not that I know. Sugar, Debs?'

She ignored the coffee and glowered at Naylor. She said, 'Were you in Northern Ireland?' Now the accusation was edging into her tone.

'No.'

'No? And how did you manage that?'

'He's just born lucky,' said Paul, embarrassment creeping into his voice. Irene and Ruth started a quiet polite conversation ignoring the situation.

Naylor said, 'No, I was not born lucky, I was born in Westmuir Street in the East End of Glasgow. Second youngest of five brothers and two sisters. My da still works in the meat market with two of my brothers. The others are on the dole which is where I'd be if – '

'Spare me the broken heart!' She stood up. 'Excuse me, I'm leaving!'

Paul said, 'Dear God, Debs!' and pursued her out of the living room.

Ruth sighed. Irene squirmed. Naylor felt like making a few very rude gestures, instead he rose, nodded with what he imagined was some gallantry to the ladies and strolled off in Paul's wake.

Paul was pleading with her on the porch, holding

her elbow. 'Look,' he was saying, 'I'll drive you back to the camp. You can't walk all that way in the middle of the night.'

'Just bloody well leave me alone!' She yanked her arm free and strode off.

'Debs!'

'Sorry, Paul.' Naylor slapped him on the shoulder as he walked past. 'You were right – don't socialise with the clientele.'

She was striding out along the shore road by the time he manoeuvred the Nova along side her. He'd taken his time. Why rush? She wasn't going to outpace him and a little cooling off period was in order anyway. So ten minutes after her dramatic exit he slowed to walking speed slightly ahead of her and on the other side of the road. What should he say? Say nothing. Stay Captain Cool here in the driving seat. Roll top rolled down. Wee bit of Vivaldi on the tape player. See if she rises to it.

She shouted, 'Go to hell, Naylor!'

Naylor smiled and put the boot down. The Nova took off down the road and he turned up left out of her sight, found a quiet little residential street and killed the lights. He gave it ten more minutes and then went after her again.

This time she was walking on the left side of the road and not quite so vigorously. He pulled up ahead of her and opened the passenger door. This was a gamble. She might kick it shut and damage the paint work, even with her trainers. But she climbed in, closed the door and sat there saying nothing, arms folded, face in a frown.

'Didn't you say there were hundreds of people with armed forces backgrounds in the Peace Movement? That's what makes you so credible? Why the sudden change in attitude to me, then?'

'You're a plant, Naylor. You're working for bloody MI5.'

'Know what I did in the Army?'

'Tell me, please. In charge of the Naafi? Or a pay clerk perhaps or – '

'I was a captain in British Army Intelligence seconded to Nato and spent the years prior to resigning my commission stationed in Berlin and West Germany.'

She looked at him, stared hard.

'Some joke,' she said.

'I was having a drink with some mates one night in Hamburg. It was a waterfront bar that had been converted into a club, quite snazzy, always a good supply of interesting ladies. Anyway we left about three in the morning but I went back for my wallet and there was this god fucking almighty explosion. Car bomb. They'd been waiting for us. Bits of human bodies and Rover 2000 everywhere. Absolutely unbelievable. The kind of experience that turns your head right round three hundred and sixty degrees. I decided to make war no more. So here I am.'

For a few moments she sat staring at him and then she said, 'Who was it?'

'IRA. Provos laid claim to it. Nobody established precisely who actually did it.'

'My God.'

'That was the only time I saw any so-called "action". I never went to Belfast or Port Stanley. That is not the kind of life for me. To paraphrase the T-shirt; see the world, travel to exotic places, meet fascinating people and get killed by them. No. Thanks.'

'And you don't work for MI5.'

'I don't. I work for Munro Kerr Meikle, the largest

of the old Glasgow law firms. They are my sole and solitary paymasters.'

He looked into the smart grey eyes. He was telling the truth. The information he passed on went only to the Ministry of Defence and for this consideration he was less than adequately remunerated. How good, Naylor wondered, were her psychic powers?

'Take me home, please.'

'Perhaps a coffee and a small brandy back at mine?'

She shook her head. 'No. I mean, maybe. But some other time.'

There was something irrational about waking stone cold sober and suspiciously healthy on a Sunday forenoon. Naylor liked it. It was bizarre. He drove along a bright near deserted Dumbarton Road, the car windows rolled down and Brandenburgs streaming from his tape player, Leppard giving them big licks with the English Chamber Orchestra. Brilliant!

By the time he came off the Expressway the traffic had thickened. Families piling into the city centre Sunday markets. Ten years ago there was just the Barras and a couple of shops open. These days the city was alive from just past the Anderston Bus Station right through to Bridgeton which was where Naylor drew his red line. Further east he would not go. Further east was Parkhead, Shettleston, Tolcross – everything he had aspired so hard away from.

The car park facing onto the black glass Lubianka of the old Express building was full so he parked in College Street and strolled round to the Turkish café.

It was bright and busy. The young Turk and a

middleaged woman raced from counter to table calling orders through the cowboy-style swing doors to the kitchen. A row of functional plastic topped tables and chairs extended back to the set of wooden booths, a relic of older if not better days.

The back booth, the one facing the far wall was the only one with a single occupant.

Naylor weaved his way to the table and eyed the man. There was mass of unkempt black hair which might have been curly with frequent applications of brush and soapy water, an equally untidy and straggly beard. The face was lean, underfed, with pale blue organstop eyes and a projecting upper lip. Long bony fingers linked round a fresh cappucino.

Naylor said, 'Mr Haggerty?'

'They do a nice big chunky joint of lamb wi' rice and pitta bread for about three fifty. And more coffee. You should try the Turkish coffee. Keep ye awake for a fortnight. No kidding.' The voice was soft but hoarse, good for whispering.

As Naylor squeezed into the booth beside him the Turk zoomed in for the order. Naylor ordered Haggerty's suggested lunch for them both.

'If I talk to you it's confidential and that, right? Like, y'know, talking to a priest?'

'Only if you're a client and it's relevant to your case.' And, Naylor thought, if you're going to tell me something worthwhile on the Lexie Beattie murder I'm going to cite you as a witness.

Haggerty's face twisted about, digesting the information. Then it twisted to one side in a wee tight-lipped smile that showed no teeth and he said, 'Aye well, maybe,

73

maybe no. Fine. I'll fill you in on some wee pointers, pal.'

'You said on the phone you were getting me vetted.'

'No offence, pal. Canny be too careful these days. Know what I mean? Eh?'

'How did you get me vetted? Have you got contacts in Kentigern House?'

Haggerty snorted. 'MoD? You're joking. Naaa. More ways of skinning the cat.'

'Uh huh. So you're with some kind of hand knitted organisation. You and some of your "pals".'

His eyes narrowed and he stiffened a little. 'We are the underground. The real underground.'

Naylor smirked. 'I like that – the Glasgow underground. What do you call yourselves, the Inner Circle, or is it the Outer Circle?'

'Oh that's very good. I didn't realise you were a wit, Mr Naylor. Sir.'

'So what's your group called? I do like to know who I'm dealing with.'

'APG.'

'Oh. Well well. The good old Army of the Provisional Government of Scotland. And here was me thinking you boys all wound up doing time.'

'Keep your voice down, will ye? That was years ago. We're totally reformed, new membership, new leadership, the lot. And nearly every one of us has seen action!'

'But not all in the paras like you, Mr Haggerty.'

'Oh. Who told you?' Standing and looking up over the back of the booth, eyeing the clientele, the street outside.

'Why did you leave? Conscience?'

'Naw.' He sat down. 'Chucked me out when they found I was a member of the International Socialists.'

'They can be narrow minded that way,' Naylor said. 'Were you at Lexie Beattie's flat the day she was murdered?'

'Better than that. I found her. See that "anonymous person" that raised the alarm? Me.' He tapped his right forefinger to his chest and grinned a big yellow-grey dental nightmare. 'What about that then, eh? Big surprise? Eh? Eh?'

'What were you doing there?'

'Visiting, wasn't I? I mean when they say she was a militant they're spot on. I can guarantee that, pal. Met her at one of them 1320 Club do's. She was right into my line of thinking. Nobody gives freedom away – you've got to kick it out the fuckers, 'scuse my Swahili. But the one that kicks longest's the one that kicks last. She found that out. Eh?'

'A minute. I'm trying to straighten this out in my head. You're telling me she was a member of the APG?'

'Naaw. Look, pal, clean your ears out, will ye? I'm saying I was her contact wi' the APG. Me. Comprenday? I passed on a lot of info to her, some real red hot gen. When I was goin' up the close I saw these two characters beltin' down the stairs. Goin' like the clappers. And they had kit bags. Navy style kit bags. Nearly sent me flyin' so they did. Now, I never saw them comin' out her door but they were in there. And I think I know who they were. And I think I know the do-cu-ments what they were lookin' for.'

Two plates piled with lamb, rice and pitta bread were pushed in front of them. Haggerty attacked his with a drooling excitement.

'Okay, Haggerty, I'm interested. Who were they and what were they after?'

But Haggerty was on a food high. He mumphed through a stuffed mouth and indicated that Naylor should commence the proper business of lunching. Naylor sighed and started to eat. It was better than he'd expected but he really wasn't here to Egon Ronay the place. After a few minutes Haggerty's plate was clear and he was into his second cappucino.

'Now, that's what I call a real treat. Know what I mean. Total brilliant, man.'

'So who were they?'

'Heard of SB Services? What am I talkin' about? Course you have.'

Naylor nodded. 'Some kind of security company?'

Haggerty smirked. 'Aye, some kind, right enough eh? Sneaky Beakies …'

Naylor frowned. 'That's the nickname for the Special Boat Squadron, isn't it?'

'Aye aye, captain. Right first time.'

'You mean they're ex-SBS?'

Haggerty gave him a long look. 'Tellin' me you don't know, pal? Really'n truly, cross yer heart'n hope to die?'

Doubt flickered in Naylor's mind. 'Should I?'

Haggerty raised his eyebrows and shrugged and said, 'The most a them's ex-marines but they take in a lot from the Army too.'

'Hold on. Let me get this clear in my head, Haggerty. You're saying that the two characters you saw were SB Services people. I don't follow this at all.'

'SB Services are experts at "dirty tricks" operations, pal. Their so-called security expertise includes bodyguard work, training people in anti-terrorist techniques, setting up private armies for the odd sheik or African dictator here and there. That's the above board bit. They also do some definitely under the counter contract work home and away for certain Whitehall departments and a few big companies. Heard rumours they did some consultancy work for the drug barons. How to slip your boat through the Florida Keys and juke past the Coast Guard and the FDA choppers. That's supposed to be a wee bit on the side. The side Her Majesty's got her blind eye on. Wink wink nudge nudge, know what I mean? Eh?'

Naylor sighed, 'Oh, I see. It's a conspiracy theory is it? Wonderful. Lexie Beattie was murdered by Downing Street because she had abusive letters about the government published in the *Times*.'

'Naw, she only wrote to the big London papers.'

'I'm talking about the London *Times*, not the *Evening Times*.'

'Uh, anyway that's not what they killed her for. They were looking for something.'

He smirked and drained the coffee.

Naylor groaned. He said, 'Well? You do intend telling me what they were looking for?'

Haggerty pulled a face. 'Oooh. Dunno. See its a wee bit hush hush and that. Only for the ears of those and such as those as it were.'

'Haggerty, you are an extremely frustrating person.'

'Wife said that. Went off wi' a plumber. Came to fix the lavvy and she buggered off wi' him. Mind you he was a tradesman.'

'Goodbye, Mr Haggerty.'

'C'mere, c'mere. Listen I'm going to tell you. Okay. Right. Ever heard of *Clawback*?'

Naylor shook his head. 'No,' he said. 'Should I have?'

'You might. Anyway. It's a military plan of action for what's to be done come independence.'

'Come independence? I don't follow.'

'Mister Naylor, I am talking about what the English Armed Forces are supposed to do in the event of Scotland gaining independence. If we go UDI, y'know like Rhodesia did.'

'And this *Clawback* is an outline of London's military response to a Scottish UDI?'

Haggerty cleared his throat and began, '*Clawback* is a detailed plan for isolatin' all oil and nuclear interests in Scotland, both civil and military, in the event of independence. It also covers sensitive military areas committed to America and NATO. Some other bits and pieces too. Like all the major airports, all the big electronics operations. They're even supposed to uproot a few thousand key workers and academics and all their equipment and magic carpet them over the border. The APG have a copy of the latest version of this wee scheme. And we gave Lexie Beattie a photostat of it.'

He sighed and sat back as if he'd just accomplished something major and very difficult. He had said it all so fluently, flawlessly, that Naylor realised he'd practised it many many times before.

'Very interesting. The place had certainly been ransacked. That would account for it.'

'Lexie wouldn't've given them bugger all without a fight. They beat the crap out her and left her for dead when she said nothin.' Then they tore the house to bits lookin' for the goods. Good ol' Sneakey Beakey Services, eh? They're your killers, Mr Naylor.'

Five:Rallentando

HE DROVE WEST out of the city musing on how to find Haggerty.

It had not come as a surprise when the ex-para had "gone to the toilet" and not returned. Naylor had sat reading the incredibly bad press the peace movement was being given over this affair. The *Sunday Mail* had LEXIE MUR-DERED baldly on the front page with a black edged colour portrait. *Scotland on Sunday* had a picture of her and one of Debs Mooney over their front page lead. There were articles in all the Sundays. Some features speculated on the peace organisations being corrupted and manipulated by outside influences. None of it was going to do Naylor's client one spit of good.

What Naylor needed was a witness like Haggerty but Haggerty had no intention of standing up and pointing the proverbial finger in court. He was driven by an anglophobia keenly focused to a seething hatred of the British Army. He was also a key witness. Might even be the actual murderer, although Naylor doubted it: there seemed no point to his statement unless he was either a sensation seeker or was really involved in some way.

CHAPTER FIVE

Tomorrow he would phone Hasties, the private detectives used by MKM. They could do a trace and check him out. It should be straightforward enough. Haggerty was undoubtedly on the dole. Hasties would just tell the DHSS that he was wanted for aliment payment and they'd probably cough up the address.

He crossed the Erskine Bridge, took the coast road down to Largs and left the Nova in the big car on the front. Then he went for a stroll.

For Naylor this town was sweet and sour. As a boy he had come here on annual day trips to the seaside with his brothers and sisters. The beach was all shale and pebbles but there were the donkey rides and the thrills of throwing stones into the sea and at one another.

It had not been a happy childhood. That was the sour part. Five boys and two girls sharing a room and kitchen with their parents, sharing an outside toilet with two other large families on the same floor. Mammy, a shrill matriarch, tall and skinny and with the good looks of her Black Irish forebears. Da, ineffectual and drunk and violent, a meat market porter with a reputation as a 'hard man.' Once Mammy's brother had a shouting match with him, about wife-beating and Da punched him so hard he smashed right through the kitchen door and spent ten days in the Royal. Of such stories were family legends made.

The sweet memories returned by Largs were quite literally sweet. Nardini's Café was a special treat from Auntie Ina, his mother's sister-in-law, a high tea with cream cakes and what had to be the best ice cream in the world. God, how he'd glutted himself. Sick on the train home and worth every spasm. But those annual visits ended when Ina's husband landed in the lobby with a broken jaw and the remnants of the kitchen door around him.

Today it was noisy, a funfair blazed and roared like a mad steelworks, frustrating car filled roads, streets swilled with guzzlers of cola, lager, irn bru, gorging on candyfloss, hotdogs, chips, toffee apples, burgers, you-name-it. Weans bobbing with big metallic balloons, mothers screaming and skelping, fathers harassed or bored or toting toddlers on their shoulders. And through the crowds dogs yelping, old folk shuffling arm in arm, teenagers shrieking, mechanical monkeys telling incomprehensible jokes, barkers wheedling, curses, shouts and laughter. Smells of fried food, fish and frankfurters and onions and underlaid with an iodine-ozone whiff of sea water carried on the chill breeze coming in across the long lazy rush of waves.

Naylor looked out at the Millport car ferry coming in and noticed its lights. Sky was shading fast into gloaming. He'd been wandering around for hours in a dream.

Nice.

Opting for an espresso with Perrier on the side and an open turkey sandwich in Nardini's, he listened to the small orchestra move through a selection of fifties' favourites. Only the electronic signboard advertising various local services and luxuries stopped the scene from being a total timewarp. Naylor was happy.

There were four messages on his answering machine. Two were from police informing him they had custodies who wanted him to represent them. One was from Iain Gray on the *Glasgow Herald* who asked him to call back before seven so it was too late for that. The last from Big Bill Nicholson, a polite request to 'phone him soonest, dear boy.'

Big Bill's voice was as avuncular as ever. Naylor could see the white dinner jacket, the library of that large house on the outskirts of Kilbirnie. Bill would be leaning back in the red leather club chair, a post-prandial brandy and port on the table beside him, log fire crackling away. Fresh lit Havana in the thick well manicured fingers. That was the way Naylor always thought of him, bearing all the trappings of affluence and power. He couldn't conceive of the man in a pair of battered bedroom slippers, in an elderly Shetland sweater with patches on the elbows, hunched over a stack of files in his small dishevelled study, a cracked glass ashtray crammed with butts beside a mug of weak Sweetexed tea under the reading light.

'I believe you've had a recent social encounter with Sheriff Forbes, among others.' Was there a snifter of suppressed humour in those words?

'I made an absolute idiot of myself on Friday night, Bill.'

'Perhaps the Friday nights are getting a trifle out of hand, Jack. There have been other reports, you know.' Jee-zuz! Have there, indeed? And who has been snitching on Jackie Naylor? Lambie? It could be anyone. Naylor had come to regard Scotland as the kingdom of the brown-nose. The country of the clipe and the backdoor gossip.

'Are they? Oh. Well, I think I'm ready for an extended period of abstemiousness, anyway.'

'The Partners know, of course. I was actually informed over dinner last night at the Western. I imagine you're going to find a whole lot of little remarks and smiles grace your presence in and around the courts for some time to come.'

'I'm a bit worried about the Law Society's

attitude – '

'Good God, don't be such an imbecile, dear boy. Absolutely no chance of anything happening there. How you disgrace yourself in your own time is your affair. And if anyone should say otherwise I'll put the boot in. Shan't I?'

'Well, that's a relief.'

'But I do expect you to moderate your alcohol intake over the next few months, Jack. For your own good.'

'I won't touch another drop till Hogmany.'

'Oh, let's say Christmas Eve. Nothing wrong in being festive at the appropriate time.'

'Hah ha, right, er … Right, Christmas Eve then, Bill.'

There was a short pause before Big Bill spoke again. The tone had changed. Much smoother, chocolatey …

'You've never been involved in a murder trial before have you, Jack?' What kind of question was that? Was Nicholson thinking of putting someone else in? Not a chance. Banks had expressly asked for yours truly, Jackie Naylor and unless he specifically wanted to change that, Jackie Naylor would be on the case.

Naylor said, 'I actually have another one on the go.'

'Oh, you mean that wife killing her husband thing? No, I mean a real scorcher like this one.'

'Well, this is certainly going to give me some much wanted experience.'

'Hmmmm. This is a rather sensational not to say unsavoury affair, don't you think?'

'Unsavoury? Well, its murder so – '

'Precisely. Murder. Violence. Press and television and all that sordid nonsense. Especially with that woman. Almost makes one dizzy just contemplating what might occur.'

'Well, what is it they say in Hollywood? "There's no such thing as bad publicity"?'

'Quite. Hollywood. And I think we'd certainly agree that for all its melodrama the High Court is hardly that.'

'But, I mean surely we have to pursue this. I've done High Court cases before: GBH, rapes, robbery – '

'Of course, of course you have. And there is no doubt whatsoever that you've dealt with them all admirably. You are a very professional person, Jack. No that's not what I'm suggesting at all.'

'Then … what are you suggesting? That I get the charge reduced to culpable homicide or – '

'No, er. Well it really is quite a delicate matter. I really do not think that this is the kind of case that MKM can really afford to be associated with, if you follow me.'

'No, I don't follow you. I don't follow you at all. This is one of the biggest things to come my way. It's going to be a major legal case. So what are you saying?'

'What I am trying to express, dear boy, is the fact that the Partners will expect you to keep the firm's name out of the press. We are an old, established and … mature. I'm quite certain that some of our major clients would look askance at us becoming involved in a media circus. No, this matter must be dealt with swiftly and with a degree of tact.'

'You mean that some of those big cats you represent like Kromar and Dominion Oil might prefer to take their business to a firm with a lower profile?'

'A rather grave risk, I fear. And not one we should be willing to take. I have conferred with the Partners on this. They agree.'

'Oh.'

'Now in the circumstances what I recommend is that you talk to this Mr Banks and encourage him to plead guilty.'

'What?'

'Easiest way out. Now, I'm sure you must see that. The police have provided the Crown with an excellent case – '

'How do you know?'

'I beg your pardon?'

'How do you know what kind of case they've got? The Crown? I mean this is Sunday night. Right? The Crown won't so much's get their sniff of this until tomorrow. How can you say – '

'Calm down, dear boy, calm down. Don't upset yourself so. I had to pop across to my Edinburgh club this afternoon, committee meeting, you know. Well, I bumped into a chum from the Crown Agent's office and apparently they've all been up to high-doh on this – '

'Whaaaat …?'

'Ah, precisely. There's something enormously fishy going on at the crossroads here, my boy. I wouldn't be at all surprised if something quite revolting should manifest itself if this laundry be given a thoroughly public washing. And I'm sure you must see that this would hardly prove to be in anyone's interests.'

'What about the interests of justice?'

'You're being tiresome now, Jack.' All avuncularity edged from the voice. 'Have him kick a plea.'

'Well, I think this man has a good case as a matter of fact and I do not in all conscience see how I can do that.'

'Sleep on it. Perhaps it might be worth passing it over to someone in another firm with a good reputation in criminal matters. Joe Beltrami, for example. Think it over.

And remember, Jack, you were recommended by an old friend. I wouldn't like to tell him that things weren't working out with you any longer. As I said, sleep on it.'

The phone went dead. Naylor hung up.

What was going on? "Recommended by an old friend"? The MoD? Did they have an interest in this? But how? Was Haggerty right? Had the MoD hired SB Services to lift the *Clawback* document? Had they topped Beattie in the process right enough? Maybe they wanted Banks to take the rap for it and draw attention away from themselves? Jee-zuz, what a mess.

He popped open the MFI teak-effect drinks cabinet and snatched out a one third full bottle of Absolut, dumped himself on the pine futon/sofa and took a big swig from the neck. He felt no better. Another swig. Fumbled around for the TV remote control. And what was all that preamble about the Friday nights? Was his drinking supposed to be tied into the Lexie Beattie affair? You'll only get Big Bill protecting your drink habit if you toe the line?

Television was showing a film about men in a submarine. They were being hunted, depth-charged. He knew how they felt. The memory of the Hamburg car bomb car bomb shuddered briefly through him.

Another swig.

In his thick Liverpudlian Banks said, 'No. I didn't do it. Did I? So I'm not going to plead guilty to it, am I? I'd have to be totally brain-dead to do something stupid like that.'

Naylor said, 'Then I'm not sure I can take this on. If you insist on your innocence I think I'll have to step out the picture.'

'You mean I'll have to get another lawyer. Why?'

'Look, Alan. I've no experience in handling this kind of case. I just have no track record. You need someone who can properly represent you.'

'Don't tell me what I need, Mr Naylor. I know what I need alright. Someone who is sympathetic to our cause. That's what. You've put in far more time with us than we'd have got from anybody else. We're not total cretins, you know. We have noticed. I know your heart's with us. Don't you see, that's what counts?'

'Well, look there's that other lawyer, the one who advises the Faslane peace-camp ...'

'What? The Angel of Dunkenny Square? That crazy woman from Drumchapel? Not a chance.'

'Then she must be crazy the right way. Miss Mullane gets great results any time I see her in court.'

'But that's not the point. I know you. I trust you. I know I can totally rely on you. And at this time, which is the most difficult time in my life ever, I need all that. I don't need chopping and changing and tearing down our whole two year relationship just to build up another from scratch. I'm counting on you to come through for me. Do you really believe I killed her? Well, do you?'

Naylor sighed though his mouth and turned away. The cell was as depressing as ever, magnified tenfold by his throbbing hangover. He swallowed and tasted dead flies in old mould. He needed a drink.

Banks pressed him further. 'Come on, do you believe it? Do you honestly think I did in Lexie Beattie?'

'That's not the issue here – '

'No. Wrong. That is the only issue here. That's the only relevant thing we have to look at right now. Well? No. You don't believe it, do you? Go on admit it. Look yourself

CHAPTER FIVE

in the eye. Do you think I killed that old woman? Yes or no?'

Naylor shook his head.

'See,' said Banks. 'I didn't think you did.'

'Unfortunately I am a junior partner in an old established law firm and they don't give a hoot about my opinions on this matter one way or the other. They don't want the firm's name associated with the scandal in any way. They've told me to get out of it.'

'Tell them to stuff it.'

'Easy to say. Not quite so easy to do. They are just as likely to tell me to go take a walk out the door.'

'Then do it. You'll get all the publicity you need to set up yourself if they do. Even if they don't. I mean a big trial like this is going to give you a lot of exposure.'

'Not really. I don't appear for you in the High Court. That'll be an advocate. I've got one, thank God. He'll be making the big defence.'

'Yes, but you put the case together, all the facts and things like that.'

'Well, yes, but – '

'And you can always have a lunch here or there with the odd lady or gentleman of the press just to fill them in, unofficially of course, on any old developments behind the scenes.'

'That would be frowned upon – '

'God, it's your career, man. Don't be a fish about it. Go for it.'

The sudden turn of the conversation surprised and alarmed Naylor, rather like having your morning swim and someone dumps a killer shark in the pool.

'My career is my business – '

'And my life is mine. How long am I going to go down for? Eight years? Ten? Well, that's at least as important to me as your bloody career.'

'Look, I can just walk out of here. Right now. Just leave you thrashing around looking for someone else. Or I can find someone who can do a much better job of this than I can. Or you can plead guilty. Those are your options.'

Banks' voice went very low, almost a growl. His gaze shifted to Naylor's scuffed grey Hush Puppies. 'You drop me in it and I'll do the same right back, mate. Walk out on me now and I'll make the biggest stink I can cook up. I'll try everything. The press, the Law Society, my bloody MP, I don't care.'

Eyes bunched and voice rumbling to a growl he stared at Naylor. 'Know what I'll do? I'll say that every time I appeared in court up to now you told me what story I was to yap on the witness stand. And this time you're refusing. Backing away. They won't like that. Will they?'

Naylor winced. It was like realising someone was tickling your jugular with the point of a hunting knife. The fact it was really a tapestry of lies mattered not a damn.

Banks went on, 'I'll scream it from the bloody rooftops. Some way some day its going to stick and then you're really going to be in trouble. Your precious bloody old school tie law firm will get shot of you so fast you'd think you'd AIDS! Then you'll be the one who's thrashing around only this time the publicity won't exactly be what every lawyer dreams about. Oh no. It's going to be your worst nightmare come true. And I never bluff. Ask Debs or any of them. Never. I really mean it, Mr Naylor!'

Way down in deep waters, being depth charged, killer sharks closing in, it was a nightmare already. Turn one way Big Bill was going to hammer you. Turn the other and Banks would just lie in his teeth and scream blue murder. Naylor leaned his head against the cold wall and closed his eyes. Banks was waiting, quiet now he'd said his piece. What was it in that conversation with Big Bill last night? Whose interests had to be served? A tiny patch of light appeared high above through the murky waters. Yes, the interests of justice. Doing the Right Thing. Make a change.

'Okay then, we do it your way, Alan. Not Guilty.'

'Did I ever tell you, you're a wonderful person?' And he threw his giant arms around Naylor, stunned him in a bear-hug.

'Ooomph,' said Naylor.

Six:Da Capo

L UNCH IN THE ROGANO Oyster Bar was a treat Naylor relished every time he spent midday in the city. Smoked salmon sandwiches and a few glasses of white wine, crisp, French and always brilliant. His personal opinion about the origins of the New Glasgow were that it had germinated here in the years before the Second World War.

The decor was sophisticated Thirties. The service came from another era, another planet. The ambience of cosmopolitan elegance and urban energy thrilled Naylor. When he moved into MKM's St. Vincent Place offices he'd lunch here daily. No longer the most junior partner out in the sticks. By then he'd have a more upmarket residence, of course, maybe a chic wee patio flat on the south bank of the Clyde overlooking the river. Maybe he'd marry, a classy female like Melanie Forbes would be *de rigueur*, move down to the Ayrshire coast, get a few nice acres and a view of Arran, couple of healthy boys, deerhound, some peacocks in the garden ...

John, the essence of Rogano, leaned across the bar and said, 'Your office on the phone for you, sir.'

Naylor sighed. So much for escape. He'd tried clearing his head of this morning's snash. Defending a client, one of three up on an armed robbery charge. Stoned half blind they phone a taxi to pick them up from home. They take it to a bank. They try tanning the bank. What kind of people go by taxi from home to a hold up?

It was the voice of Annie Burns. 'Mr Nicholson is out for your blood. I don't think Banks put in the right plea this morning. That's the impression I get. Anyway you've to phone his nibs at St Vincent Place. He's staying in through lunch to wait for your call. Must be serious. Okay? Right, that cop phoned. Flanagan. Says he'll meet you in a couple of minutes. Sounds dodgy to me. I think he's Special Branch.'

'So do I.'

'Helluva dodgy people. You sure you want to see them?'

'No choice, Annie. It's to do with the Lexie Beattie thing.'

'Aye, well be polite. Never come to the attention of the authorities. That's what my da used to say.'

'I promise to be well behaved.'

'That'll make a change from Friday night.'

'Pardon?'

'I said that'll make a change from Friday night. You're the talk of the steamie.'

'God. How did you find out?'

'Three guesses.' That meant Bobby Turner, his assistant.

'Has that wee shit been blabbing to everybody?'

'He's been on the phone to all his pals half the morning spreading the glad tidings.'

92

'I'm going to take this higher. I want him out of that office. This is the last bloody straw I – '

'Hold your horses just a wee minute. Do you remember the photographs?'

'Photographs? What are you talking about?'

'Aye, I thought as much. Well, listen, he's telling everybody that there was a whole lot of pictures taken of you and your high jinks.'

'You're kidding!'

Then he remembered climbing out of Lambie's car at the Maltings and Lambie slipping a new camera into his pocket. Big shite!

'And he's getting a set of prints of his own to show around.'

'Jee-zuz. Oh, I think I'm going to be sick.'

'Well get cleaned up before you see those police.'

The two detectives took up stools beside him at the bar so soft he almost missed their arrival. Flanagan ordered a plate of smoked salmon sandwiches and a white wine spritzer.

'Nice weather for September, Mr Naylor,' said the small one with the red hair, the pimply white face and the evil eyes. 'Indian summer, maybe?'

'Seen much of the Culture City events, Jack?' said Flanagan. 'That shipbuilding extravaganza their doing in Govan looks good. Did somebody tell me they're actually going to be launching a real ship?'

And so they chatted a while and then like fish sliding from river to sea, they casually moved to the cold deeper waters: Lexie Beattie's murder.

'Cranstonhill got an anonymous tipoff around, oh,

I think it was four thirty eight. They were on the scene at
four forty four.' He was reading from the lilac pages of his
Filofax.

'Mmmm, four minutes. I'm impressed, Flan. When
did you appear on the scene?'

'Hold your horses, Jack. All in good time. They
found the doors of Mrs Beattie's flat wide open and the
house an utter shambles. In the kitchen they found herself
lying by the sink. She was evidently in a critical state. The
anonymous caller had also alerted the ambulance service
and an ambulance arrived at eight minutes past five. A
woman police constable went with her to the Western
Infirmary's Casualty Department. Then to the Intensive
Care unit where Lexie Beattie died at twenty three minutes to
seven – at which point this became a murder investigation.'

Flanagan's monotone rolled on describing the state
of the flat on the police arrival. It matched Naylor's notes
exactly. Except that there had been a pile of ashes in the
kitchen sink which had been well mashed and stirred with
water. According to Flanagan this was still being examined
by a forensic team. Preliminary results indicated that it may
have been a large list of some kind.

Naylor noted the names of the uniformed officers
who were first on the scene. He'd go over their statements
very carefully indeed.

Next door neighbour heard banging and shouting
but did not know if the noise was coming through the wall
or from upstairs. Yes, she saw Banks leaving the close. No,
she could not say whether the banging began before or after
his departure. Had she seen anyone else entering or leaving?
No. Only the police.

Another policewoman, one not involved in the

murder investigation, remembered seeing someone fitting
the neighbour's description of Banks having a loud argument with a woman in a Land Rover around quarter past
four. She claimed to have heard the woman in the vehicle
shout several times about "that Beattie bitch."

At a quarter past seven Banks was sighted in Ban-
nisters public house by a police officer who had called in
to buy cigarettes. Several plainclothes police officers then
kept him under observation while investigations continued.
Haggerty consumed twelve pints of lager between seven
twenty five and eleven thirty five. During this time he was
heard to make a number of statements about Lexie Beattie.
He claimed that she had "sold her soul and her country short
right to the very end", that she "had always wanted to take
control of anything she got involved in" and "had never
been happy unless she had everyone at everyone else's
throat".

These were direct quotes. Banks had been talking
about her in the past tense. He was arrested on leaving the
pub at eleven thirty five.

DI Flanagan and DS Rose had come on the scene at
six the following morning to work with the forensic team
on investigation of the locus. It was obvious that a search
had been made on the premises but it was not clear if
whomsoever had made it had found what they were looking
for so Flanagan and Rose had started their own search. They
removed a number of unspecified items from the flat.

'What items did you remove?'

Flanagan said, 'Come on, Jack. If any are to be
retained as productions they'll be on the list when you see
it. We've not completed our examination of these materials
yet and so far nothing we have come across has any bearing

that we can establish.'

'And what about her files? Her lists of contacts? Her private correspondence?'

'It is all being examined for relevance.'

Naylor grinned at Flanagan. He felt warmly roguish with the wine in him. 'There'll be a moderate supply of political dynamite in there. Quite a wee windfall for Special Branch. But of course you won't be copying any of the information for your own use, I suppose? Very idea.'

Rose leaned towards him and said, Naylor, anyone ever tell you you're a bit of a plug, my friend?' He turned and sat side facing Naylor at the bar. 'You want to know how come we're involved in this? We'll I'll tell you, off the record of course. We had a lot of time for Lexie Beattie. She had been passing information on to us for over fifty years!'

'What?'

Flanagan chuckled. 'Since before the Second World War. That one caught you out.'

'You mean she was a plant? Jee-zuz.'

Rose frowned. 'How come you people always see things in those terms? I mean to you it's always clean cut and dried. You watch too many mini-series on tele. Too many action movies and spy films. Nothing is simple.'

Flanagan leaned forward. He said, 'Let me clarify the words of my colleague for you, old son. Lexie Beattie was a committed pacifist above and before everything else. She was a leftie, no argument, but she did not believe in violent revolution. She – '

'Are you kidding? She was into all that stuff. Seed of the Gael, the 1320 Club, Ceartas. Everybody knew that.'

Flanagan shook his head. 'Listen, Jack, and I'll tell you a story. When Lexie Beattie was in her early twenties she went to a socialist youth camp in Germany. She fell in love with some young bolshie firebrand. Germany was full of them in those days. This was 1932. Well, it seems she got engaged to this guy but she'd to come back to St Andrews to finish her degree. Something like that. Anyway this fiancé of hers worked away with a core of anti-fascists and they did serious damage to Herr Hitler's image. In November 1932 things got so bad in the elections that the Nazis were struggling for credibility. So they took over the radio and the press to a great extent. Used private life scandals to compromise big political opponents and used their street militia, their brownshirts, to take care of the small fish. One of those small fish was her fiance. He was a shipping clerk. Left his office one night to go back to his rooms. Vanished. No trace. Never seen or heard from again. She looked for him. She came back the next summer and went round all their old haunts, talked to friends and acquaintances. Nothing. Of course she was told that it was commonplace, a disgrace. But nobody was doing anything about it and that must've been what got her back up. She started going to Nazi rally's and functions and things like that.'

'Whaaat ...'

'Oh, it gets even better. Over the next five years she built up a lot of contacts in the UK. Closet Nazis, sympathisers, active fifth columnists. She was brilliant. You ever seen any of those old thrillers where the gubbins that everybody's trying to get is a diary or a file or something that's got the names of all the big secret Nazi's who would have profited from Hitler winning the war? In 1938 we had all those names, all those that mattered anyway, from a sewage works chief engineer in Liverpool right up to to the Royal Family itself.'

'She's been a British Government spy since 1933?'

'I don't think we can call her a spy, Jack. She was never paid by H.M. Government. She merely passed on information. Anyway there's nothing hush hush about it. Far as I know its a matter of public record. You know, Lexie Beattie wasn't one of those bleeding hearts who whines about how everyone in this country's living in a police state. She saw government by oppression, blackmail and corruption at first hand. She experienced life in a genuine police state, the Third Reich.'

Naylor' s brain was running ahead. He said, 'And after the war she kept on passing information.'

'She kept tabs on everyone she thought would be prone to political violence, all the fringe groups involved in Scottish nationalism from the Scottish Anthem Committee to the Scottish Republican Workers' Party. Her militancy in politics was genuine enough but she did not believe in overthrowing the democratic state by violence. She preferred the ballot box to the bomb. And she put her money where her mouth was. Always.'

'And what about the APG, Flan?'

This time Rose spoke. 'What about them?'

'Was she feeding you information on them?'

'She didn't put them behind bars, Mr Naylor Sir. We did that all by ourselves.'

'I don't mean the 'seventies affair, Sergeant. I mean here and now. Today.'

They stared at him calm and silent for a few seconds. Then Rose spoke again. 'Step for a hint?'

'Haggerty?'

Rose turned to Flanagan and said, 'How long can we hold this comedian? Like if I claim him here and now

98

and I mean totally incommunicado?'

Flanagan looked at Naylor and said, 'This is going to be a longer meeting than any of us anticipated, Jack. I assume you are acquainted with the provisions of the Prevention of Terrorism Act? We are empowered to hold you for questioning for up to five days without informing a solicitor or, for that matter, anyone in the outside world.'

Naylor felt his insides loosen. Five days? Why the hell did he have to go and open his gob?

He said, 'Hey just a wee minute. What's the problem? I was approached by this Haggerty person. He claimed to have information on the Lexie Beattie murder.'

'You better get the bill for this lot,' said Rose gripping Naylor by the back of the arm. 'We're going for a wee hop up to Pitt Street, pal.'

The Pitt Street interview room was air conditioned but still stuffy. A windowless room with cheap functional furniture and a curious air of sadness.

'Tea or coffee?' asked Flanagan.

'Pardon?'

'Well. We're going to be here a while. Might as well relax and get comfy, eh?' Flanagan said as Rose walked out the room.

'What? What? Just a minute. I'm an officer of the court executing the business of the court and if – '

'Come on, Jack. You know the score. What's more you know me. This is embarrassing. Agreed? Let's get through it quickly and forget about it. And you know I respond better to sugar than vinegar, always have. It comes from all that abuse of power we're used to. Being an officer of the court cuts no cheese within these walls, only an officer of the law. Smoke?' Flanagan offered an opened ten pack of Benson & Hedges.

'I've given up.'

'Must let me in on your secret. Mind if I do?'

'What if I do mind.'

Flanagan shrugged, 'I won't.' He put his hand on the pack to retrieve it, pocket it.

'Go ahead. Regard it as my first sugar cube to you.'

Flanagan said, 'Thanks,' and drew a cigarette from the packet which he lit with a disposable lighter. He took a deep drag and smiled. 'Mrs Beattie gave us a great deal of information concerning Mr Haggerty and his friends.'

'And what about the peace campers?'

'No, Jack. Absolutely nothing. I don't think you've been listening to me properly. She only reported to us on the avowedly or potentially violent, never on anything else. Ever. They may be many things but I don't exactly see the anti-nuke brigade and the rest of the peace movement resorting to mass bloodshed. Do you? Something of conflict of interests there, eh?'

'Er, right enough.' Naylor looked round at the door. There was no sign of Rose. 'Look, Flan, maybe you can help me. Ever heard of SB Services?'

Flanagan tilted his chair back and nodded. 'What about them? By the way, in case you're interested, SB does not stand for Special Branch. We have no connection with them.'

'Never sub-contract the odd bit of work to them. The dirty stuff?'

Flanagan chuckled. 'We've been trained to do our own dirty work. All of it.'

'Really? What about when you can't get a warrant

for a phone tap and you want the calls taped. No questions asked?'

'We always get the warrants and the questions are always asked.'

'Oh aye, sure. And who are their clients, then if its not you? MI5? CIA?'

'Could be BBC for all I know or care. We've no brief to keep an eye on them.'

'And if you had you wouldn't tell me anyway. Right?'

Flanagan did not deign to answer. Instead he tried vainly to blow smoke rings.

'What's her solicitor got to say about it all?'

'We have yet to talk.'

Naylor said, 'What? Come on. It's almost five on Monday afternoon. She's been dead three days and you haven't got in touch with her solicitor?'

'We've had no joy. She does not appear to have had one.'

'And her will?'

'Mrs Beattie appears to have died intestate?'

'That place was a shambles when I got there. Are you saying you had nothing to do with the mess?'

'Nothing at all, Jack. Scouts' honour. Dibdibdib.'

'So you weren't looking for her copy of the *Clawback* documents?'

Flanagan looked at him for a moment, continuing to rock back and forth.

'Tell me about this *Clawback*, Jack.'

'A Defence document concerned with Whitehall's retaining Scotland's strategic resources, both military and economic by use of armed force in the event of a Unilateral

Declaration of Independence.'

Hah! Pipesmoke that one, sunshine.

Flanagan shrugged, 'Never heard of it.'

'Oh, I see, therefore it doesn't exist. Is that it?'

'I could not care less if it exists or doesn't exist. Sounds probable that there would be such plans. So what? I mean its no big deal.'

'Am I hearing things?'

'So what's going to happen if some newspaper does get its hands on them, Jack? There'll be a lot of prominent red faces, toilets in Westminster'll get heavily worked. Some political farts'll resign or get chopped. The plan'll be scrapped and a new one discretely drawn up. Back to the status quo.'

'So you do not love your political masters?'

'Our work is simply concerned with the security of the democratic state.' He smiled and spread his hands in a gesture of helplessness. 'We leave the complex problems like the origins of the universe and the mysteries of love to the uniformed branch.'

Rose came in carrying a tape recorder. He was followed by a police constable carrying a tray with three steaming mugs and a packet of Abernethy biscuits.

Rose said, 'Nescafé with milk all round. I hope you're going to tell us everything about Mr Haggerty. Sir.' He sat down.

So Naylor told them everything.

Seven:Allegretto

THE DUMBARTON OFFICE of Munro Kerr Meikle occupied part of what once had been a branch of the British Linen Bank. Now it was partitioned into suites of small but moderately well furnished offices. MKM was on the glass fronted door to the left as you came in from the High Street.

Naylor pushed through, tired and rumpled after a bad night. Special Branch had held him until almost three a.m. He loathed and despised them. However he intended running some day for a Tory seat somewhere in Britain under a Law and Order ticket, so philosophically he could not bring himself to loathe and despise the 'Branch as an entity. Instead he decided to loathe and despise Rose. The little bastard seemed capable of appreciating the fact that he was on their side! Represented a perversity in what surely was an otherwise commendable institution.

Annie Burns, the senior office secretary and factotum extraordinary, glanced through the open window into the reception and raised an eyebrow. The grey eyes were piercing. She snapped, 'There'll be blood spilt if you don't phone Mr Nicholson. He's going right off his tottie.'

103

Naylor grunted and swung left through the door into his office. That woman was too strong a personality, too efficient for his liking. The kind who could answer the phone and type at the same time without breaking speed or making a mistake. Files were piled on his desk and around it on the floor. He sat down and sighed. Nine oh eight a.m. Tuesday. Next weekend lay lost ahead in mists of distant promise, whereas a day of sheer hell lay before him. No way of fending off Big Bill any longer. Then there'd be the string of battered wives, shoplifters, drunk drivers, the misfits, the socially disenfranchised and all vortexing him ever deeper into the abyss of their lives. God, the thought was depressing. Roll on Friday!

From his black hide-effect document case he hauled the morning's catch of newspapers. Lexie Beattie was still on the front page of the Scottish heavies. The peace campers still taking a battering from the press. Naylor sighed and chucked them back into his case.

'Get me Head Office,' he said to Annie Burns on the phone. 'I'm ready for Big Bill, now.'

'You poor soul,' she said. Twenty seconds later a more antiseptic voice replied. He was through. 'This is Jack Naylor at the Dumbarton office. Mr Nicholson, please.'

'Oh ... Er, hold one moment.'

There was the stupid music head office used when you went on hold. The Legend of the Glass Mountain. God in Heaven.

'Er, Mr Nicholson's not available right now.' There was a pause and something muffled by a hand over the mouthpiece. 'He'll be in this afternoon, Mr Naylor.' This woman was choking back laughter and there was definite tittering in the background. 'He said you should – '

Naylor hung up.

Bugger this! He marched through the door to the office of his assistant Robert Philip Turner generally known as Wee Bobby despite continual attempts to have people call him "Phil". Naylor had always thought Wee Bobby epitomised a particular rodent sub-species of Glaswegian. His face was twitchy, furtive; beady pinkish eyes always shifting, pointed nose and no appreciable chin, mousey hair plastered flat on the scalp. Pale hands, small and nervous. The clothes a nondescript grey brown.

He flinched at the sight of Naylor.

'I want those pictures and I want the negs.' Naylor put his fist on the man's desk and leaned on them.

'Pictures? Eh, Jack, I don't know what – '

Naylor cut in quietly, 'You don't know what day of the week it is. That's what you don't know, Bobby. Let me tell you: this is wake up day. Get the pictures and the negs. If you don't I am going to forget all about the code of professional conduct and break both your bloody legs and leave you in hospital for six months. I did not spend the best part of ten years in the Army Intelligence learning to polish boots.'

Turner smirked. He was nervous but confident and not buying Naylor's bluff. 'So go ahead. I'll wind up in charge of this office after six months and you'll wind up in Barlinne with no career to come out to.'

'Don't put money on that. I've got some well placed friends. Very well placed. Even in this firm.'

'Big Bill? That's a laugh. He wants your guts for garters. No, I'd say you are on the skids, Jack. Time is running out. The jungle tom-toms are saying Big Bill phoned round the papers on Monday to let them know

MKM was out of the Beattie murder case and you've really made him look a right idiot.'

'I don't think we can work in the same office. I intend reporting your conduct to the partners at the next partnership meeting. You'd be well advised to seek employment elsewhere. Matter of fact I thought I saw an ad in the *Scotsman* last week for a qualified assistant in Caithness District. I might even write you a reference.'

'It's you that's going to need the job, not me. Anyway I like it here. Annie's got a lovely bum. I wouldn't mind getting m— '

Naylor popped him on the nose with his left fist.

Turner said, 'Ooooya!'

Naylor said, 'Bobby, you mention Mrs Burns again and I'll punch your nose so far back in your face you'll look like a fucking bulldog!'

He stepped through into the main office where Annie Burns and two typists were hard at work.

'What's the diary like?' he said.

Annie Burns looked up at him. Her face was flushed. Had she overheard? 'You're in Glasgow District at two. Macallister and Saunders, both football breaches and police assaults. The files are on your desk.' Her voice was a bit clipped. Had he upset her? Was she one of those women who preferred fighting their own battles? Probably. He sighed and went through to his own office.

He ploughed into his mountain of mail, saw two women who wanted to sue the council for dampness in their homes, tried twice again to talk to Big Bill and phoned Clydebank Police Station to arrange precognitions for three cops. By that time it was twenty past eleven and he was ready for refreshment.

'Annie, could you get us a coffee?' he shouted through the slightly open door. 'And bring in the phone book?'

When it arrived there was a Jacob's Club with it. She said nothing but it seemed he was in the good books with Mrs Burns. He bit the chocolate biscuit, slurped the sweet milky coffee and flipped through the directory.

SB Services was right at the top of the S section. South Street in Whiteinch. Not the most upmarket address, but only two minutes from the Expressway and very discreet. He dialled as he munched.

'Nine three nine two. Who is calling, please?' The voice was male, quiet and precise.

'Jack Naylor of Munro Kerr Meikle, solicitors, Dumbarton office. Could I speak to whoever is in charge, please.'

'This is the duty officer speaking. How may I help you, sir?'

'Duty officer? Really? Do you have a name?'

'I'm sorry. Its company policy not hand out names, Mr Naylor. But if you date and time record any correspondence in connection with this call which is being tape recorded the company will know you are referring to me.'

'This is bizarre. You sound like – that's not important.' You sound like the KGB, CIA, SIS. 'I am trying to follow up information I have been given pertaining to a case and I believe with regard to a case and I believe your company may be able to help with.'

'Yes?'

'Yes, I have a witness who believes he saw a couple of your employees at the locus of a crime.'

'All legal matters concerning our company or its

employees are handled through our solicitors, Mr Naylor.'

'Can you tell me if – '

'Through our solicitors, Mr Naylor. I'll transfer you to our clerical staff. Someone there will give you the number. Good day.'

'Hold on a min— ... Hello? Hello?'

'Clerical. Can I help?' A woman.

'Could you please give me the name and phone number of your solicitors?'

'One moment, sir.' She vanished. At least there was no godawful background music. Thirty seconds later she was back. 'Our solicitors are Munro Kerr Meikle, St Vincent Place – '

'What,' said Naylor. 'Did you say Munro, Kerr, Meikle?'

'Correct, sir. The gentleman to speak to is Mr William Nicholson, the – '

'What? Big Bill? Are you sure?'

'Well, of course I'm sure. Its right here in front of me. Do you want the phone number?'

Naylor dropped the phone back on the rest.

Jee-zuz. Big Bill? SB Services' lawyer?

He felt a rush of cold and he shuddered and pushed back from the desk in his chair to thump against the wall. Big Bill Nicholson? What the hell was going on here? So Big Bill wants Jackie Naylor to do a quick hands off job, to do a runner from a red hot case. Why? Just because this was not the kind of thing a snotty firm like MKM dirtied its fingers on? Or was there some other motive here?

Follow the logic chain. Beattie is murdered. An informant tells you SB Services is involved. SB Services' lawyer tries to pull you off the job. Coincidence?

Or maybe Big Bill's masters just yanked his strings?

So is MoD involved? But how? They'd never touch an outfit like SB Services with the proverbial long pole. Or would they? Is Big Bill tied into MI5? Seems unlikely considering the bad blood between them and the MoD, the jealousies, the budget squabbling and the conflicts of interest …

Naylor felt dizzy, felt like a drink. This was the ultimate cleft stick. If he didn't do what Big Bill wanted he could lose his job. If he didn't do what Banks wanted Banks could create the kind of stink that would lose him his job anyway. If Big Bill was tied into more than just the MoD there was a chance Naylor could lose more than just his job. But if he backed away and Banks made sure that bad news about Naylor spread like botulism, SB Services might be contracted to service him in any case.

No matter what way he turned he was stonewalled.

He imagined someone jumping him as he stepped into his flat at night. Or maybe they'd drive him off the road into a wall. Horror images from too many action movies exploded in his head. Flames, blood, screaming, fireballs …

The phone rang and Naylor jumped. He picked it up on the third ring and swallowed and spoke.

'Er … hello?'

It was Annie Burns. 'I've got Mr Nicholson on the other end wanting a word with you – '

'No,' he shrieked and threw the phone down. He ran. As he charged through the outer office Annie Burns shouted something about afternoon appointments.

'Get cover. Cancel everything for the next six months,' he bellowed almost falling through the door into the hallway. 'Maybe forever!'

He raced along the street, arms and legs pumping efficiently and then slowed as he approached the Nova. Car bomb, he thought and went straight away down onto his chest and began checking the underside. Remember gently, gently. Now gently, ever so gently, ease the bonnet just a crack and check it out for funny wires. Open slowly all the way. Examine the interior. Then carefully open the doors, again just a wee crack at first, explore under the seats, under the dash and in the boot.

Right. Okay. Let's go.

He was clear of the town and driving mindlessly, wallowing in the panic when he suspected he was being tailed. There was always the possibility that this was paranoia. There's a character behind on a motorcycle. Big deal. He's been there since the Nova pulled away from the parking meter. Again no big deal. Naylor gradually increased his speed putting some distance between himself and the biker. Maybe cut into Paul's cottage up at Rhu? No, God knows what kind of reception he could expect from Ruth. So he cut across to Loch Lomond. A glance in the mirror showed no sign of a pursuer. Gone? Just an innocent motorcyclist? Counting your chickens again, Naylor?

Maybe it would be a good idea to talk with Debs? At the thought of her he suddenly felt himself going hard. He snorted. Not much chance of scoring now. Still, just to have somebody to talk to about this mess. Warn her again to steer clear of the press. He nodded. Good idea. And maybe sneak back into her good books?

As he zipped past the Inverbeg Inn going north he saw the big BBC Scotland outside broadcast unit up ahead. Dread chilled and thickened in his gut. Flashing past the camp he saw a blaze of lights.

Christ, they're doing a programme!

Debs and another camper glimpsed in the doorway of one caravan. He swore and swore and beat the wheel with his fists. The car behind horned him angrily as the Nova swayed back and forth. Naylor signalled an Up Yours. Coming down Rest And Be Thankful he began growing calmer. Inveraray was ahead. Maybe he should take a breather, stop in at a pub for some lunch? The sky was leaden, darkening by the minute. Rain suddenly dumped across the landscape, across the car. The wipers slapped on and as he flicked the lights he glanced in the rear-view mirror. About a mile and a half behind there was a single light smeared on the glossed surface, a motor bike.

Fear and fascination paralysed part of Naylor's brain. The biker, the vision of some kind of leathered nemesis crouching forward on the dark machine, cutting through the rain ... Sometimes it slipped further back, vanished for a while but always returned, reappeared in the far distance.

Naylor maintained his doomwatch vigil in the mirror way beyond Inveraray. He was past Lochgilphead when he almost ran straight into a Royal Mail van. He screamed and dragged the car through a near miss. Other cars flashing and honking. Screw them. His head cleared and he saw a chance. A big semi-doubledecker bus, the German tourer type, was sitting in the Royal Ardrishaig Hotel car park. He pulled in on the far side of it, the size of the vehicle effectively screening him from the road.

Quickly he nipped out through the downpour and into the double door entrance to the hotel foyer where he waited thirty seconds brushing wetness from his chest and thighs. Then the bike shot past.

With any luck he'd go all the way to Campbeltown. Naylor allowed himself a tiny trembling smile and retired to the bar.

There was no Absolut so he forced his anxieties to dissolve in a couple of bottles of cold non-vintage Soave. They accompanied an altogether adequate lentil soup and plate of shepherd's pie and placed him in an substantially amiable mood, benign warmth flowing from his place at the bar to encompass all in the lounge.

Relaxed, smiling, Naylor savoured the feeling of cares oozing away, or as he preferred to think of it, bleeding to death. He unwrapped a Castella and ran it lovingly under his nose. He grinned as the Swan burst alight and he cupped the flame, puffing carefully, luxuriously.

'Mr Naylor.'

The biker stood there looking six foot six in his black streaming leathers and helmet, like something from a nasty science fiction movie.

Naylor's eyes popped, the cigar fell from his fingers and he began to cough convulsively almost tumbling from the barstool. The towering figure removed the crash helmet and shook free his long greasy locks. It was Haggerty.

'You led me a right merry old dance. Know what I mean, pal?'

Naylor went on coughing, his tongue protruding, face colouring rapidly.

'Where can I take these off?' Haggerty asked the woman behind the bar, indicating his jacket and rubber trousers.

'I'll show you,' she said.

Just beyond Tarbert Haggerty had realised that Naylor was off the road. What came as a surprise to him was that Naylor had been aware of the tail. Haggerty who had shrunk to a manageable five foot seven explained this as he slurped down lentil soup which was going on Naylor's bill.

'I'm definitely impressed. D'you know I've tailed Special Branch boys and they've no' clocked me. Speakin' of which, how did your wee talk wi' them go yesterday?'

Naylor sighed. He could not remember whether he had mentioned this to Haggerty. Anyway it was irrelevant. Haggerty knew.

'This is where we came in. Look, I've told you. I can't discuss this.'

'C'mon pal, I'm a witness.'

Naylor shook his head. 'You're a pain in the arse. That's all. It's the one thing the Special Branch and I both agree on.'

'So. You told them about me, eh?'

'Ah ...'

'Ah ha.'

'I've no remit to protect you, Haggerty. As far as I'm concerned you're just getting in the way.'

'Well don't blame me for you missin' court this afternoon. That's where I was told you were supposed to be. See? Findin' out things about people's dead easy, so it is. That is if there's anythin' to find out. Take your Special Branch boys for example. You think any ol' lawyer just walks in with Flanagan and Rose for a biscuit an' a wee cup of tea? Just for a social chat? Not one chance in a million years, pal. They wanted somethin' from you. Just one thing ... ' He smiled and swallowed more soup.

113

'Well, are you goin' to tell me or is the suspense supposed to kill me?'

'Me. That's what they wanted. And they wanted confirmation that my people have the *Clawback* papers. Know what they'll do now you've told them?'

'Well, not a lot according to them. They seem to be of the opinion that it does not really compromise the safety of the realm.'

At that Haggerty threw back his head and guffawed. 'Ho, you are a funny man and no mistake. A report of your conversation with them, plus a transcript, plus an analysis and the tapes of everything goes down to Curzon Street. You have heard of Curzon Street? In London?'

'The Security Service.'

'Oh my, we are posh. Just call it MI5. And once they get their dirty wee hands on it the decision's got nothin' to do wi' Strathclyde Police's Special Branch. They know that so they've got to get their homework in. Give you the full treatment. But you couldn't tell them anythin' so they had to give up after God knows how many hours tryin' to wring my address out of you, anythin'. How long – ten hours? Twelve?'

'Fourteen.'

'Silly bugger, you really are. Anyhow it's all to the good. Now I know they're still out for my blood, still followin' the trail I'm layin' for them.'

'You mean you were using me and they were using me?'

'Least I told you somethin' useful.'

'Maybe they did too.'

He smiled a row of rotten teeth and said, 'You don't mean they fed you that rubbish about Lexie bein' a

114

committed pacifist, pal? Oh ho ho.' Haggerty cackled. 'Hope they never go for a brain scan – they'll be hellish disappointed.'

'She told you about this?'

'Course she did. It was her cover, wasn't it? It's how she got herself right into the heart of Special Branch, right into the guts of the enemy. Aye, she kept us on our toes, tellin' us what they were after, where an' when, who an' how an' everythin.' Brilliant, eh? Mind you I'll tell you somethin' really valuable. You look at everythin' she wrote an' said. There's one thing, one thing that's dead cert for sure. She hated the English. God did she ever detest them! You can look that up yoursel'. She didn't like Banks. Course I gave her a wee bit of dirt there. Told her what a fascist he was in the Regiment. She could just about thole him 'cause he was workin' class. But see that snooty bitch Mooney? Hoho, no love lost there, pal.'

'Look, I know all this. Debs Mooney told me Lexie Beattie was an anglophobe.'

'Her? Well, you've no' heard the half of it. Wouldn't trust Mooney far's I could kick 'er. Mooney's all your upper class English Yawyaw. Total establishment – '

'She's Canadian, man.'

Haggerty frowned at him. 'Sometimes I think you must come from Tibet. Know that? Her family belongs to what they call the Irish Pale. That's the Protestant Irish upper class, the ones that dominated Ireland for the English Crown since the twelfth bloody century.'

'I am aware of the Pale, Haggerty.'

'Huh. Coulda fooled me, pal. What did you think her Da was? A navvy, maybe, eh? I tell you exactly what he is. He's an Oxford don, a world specialist on medieval

Music or some baloney like that. There's also a family title, his older brother's and it stretches back to the sixteenth century. Anyway, Lexie thought she was a plant, kinda fifth columnist. Y'know, MI5 F branch? The ones that put agents into targeted organisations. Remember they put yon trade unionist into the CND years ago? She told Mooney to her face an' all. "I'm going to have you thoroughly investigated, milady. Oh, yes I am!" Ho. Big ructions. Needless to say yours truly did the real investigatin' an' that. Wee word to the wise, by the way. Forget about Special Branch. They're no' interested in you or the murder. I mean how could they be? They know who done it.'

'That may not be as simple as it appears – '

Haggerty shook his head and said, 'Crap. It might've been an accident, it might no' but she was killed by the faceless men of Whitehall. Ask anybody.' He hailed a slender middle aged woman passing by. 'Hey darlin', we're havin' a wee argument. Who d'you think killed Lexie Beattie?'

She gave them both a wry look, said, 'Keep your voices down, The Powers That Be'll have your number soon enough. Hope you liked my lentil soup,' and walked off.

Haggerty shrugged and his face split into another stomach tugging grin. 'Told you. Ol' sneaky beakies. Wink wink nudge nudge. Eh?'

'All this stuff about SB Services. You thought there was some tie-in between me and them. Don't deny it.'

'Why should I? You're their lawyers.'

Naylor gaped at him and shook his head. He said, 'How in hell can you know something like that? How!'

'It's the ol' Sherlock in me an' that,' He laughed.

Naylor was going to burst in but Haggerty continued. 'Check wi' Companies House in Edinburgh. SB Services is wholly owned by Kromar PLC. An' all Kromar's interests North of the Border are represented by Munro Kerr Meikle. That's your lot or am I wrong, pal?'

Kromar, one of the world's largest multinational conglomerates. Naylor sat back making a small 'o' with his mouth. He could not have been happier if his doctor had just told him he had cancer.

Kromar.

Eight:Crescendo

HE DROVE SLOWLY past the peace camp and eyed it carefully. Two campers were sitting on folding chairs at a card table drinking tea or coffee. The weather had cleared, the wind was down and stars were peeping out. The big BBC unit was gone. No television, no reporters of any kind. Well they'd be off filing their stories by now, Naylor reasoned. He pulled the Nova into the Inverbeg Inn car park and walked back.

He was panicking these days, drinking too much, coming apart. Life, the universe and everything was getting away from him. What if Anne Burns could not arrange cover for the afternoon court? What was he going to do with Big Bill's involvement? And Kromar? Naylor felt like he had gone paddling and now there was nothing under his feet. Waters had closed over his head.

As he strolled towards the campers, hands in pockets, one of them stood. Naylor recognised him as an ex-Church of Scotland minister whose full time anti-nuclear vocation had brought his church more than a sufficiency of adverse publicity. Up until this weekend he had been the main source of Naylor's peace camp-related activity.

'Hello, Donnie, Debs around?'

'In the big caravan, Mr Naylor. She's got a journalist from *The Independent* with her.'

Naylor sighed and turned on his heel. He said, 'I don't believe this.'

'Well, it's not too bad. They're quite sympathetic, really.'

'They've got newspapers to sell just like everybody else.'

'Come on. Be fair. We have to try redressing the balance. The tabloids are murdering us. Do you know what phrase they've coined for us now? "Peace camp crazies". Now they're all using it. This is exactly the same as what happened to the Labour Party in the early eighties with the "looney left" campaign. Deliberate alienation of the public from a section of the community whose valid concerns do not meet with government approval.'

The man was just starting but Naylor had heard enough. He said, 'If she comes out within the next twenty minutes tell her I'm up the road.' He thumbed an indication at the Inverbeg Inn.

He drank four glasses of Highland Spring, iced and with lemon and then she arrived evidently high from her day of media interviews.

'Any news?' She asked sliding into the booth he favoured, the one hidden from sight of both the front window and main door. She was flushed, eyes sparkling.

'Lexie Beattie thought you were an MI5 plant in the peace movement. Want a drink?'

She gasped, 'How ... '

'How did I find out you've been lying in your teeth? Well not so much lying as gliding smoothly over some odd facts here and there. Like your supposedly Irish father's and from an old titled family and an Oxford don to boot.' Her lips became a tight line, narrow like her eyes. and Lexie Beattie detested you. "No love lost" was the way I heard it. And she thought you were an F branch plant. You do know what that is, I assume.'

Mooney nodded.

'Well? Are you?'

'You've got a damned cheek!'

'No argument there but that's not the answer I'm looking for.'

She went up to the bar and came back with a large whisky into which she poured most of a bottle of ginger ale. She sighed and began talking.

'Very well, the old bitch detested me and I her. Yes, she accused me of being an F branch plant and yes, she did have me investigated although God knows who did the investigating. The result was that she eventually came to accept the fact that I had nothing whatever to do with MI5 or MI6 or the CIA or any of those other stupid male wank fantasy organisations.'

'Was there a report of this investigation?'

'That was certainly my understanding. A few weeks ago she came up to the camp and talked at me and the others. She read from typed pages in a grey manila folder. It was humiliating, like being in boarding school again. She knew what I disliked and she enjoyed using it against me.'

'But then you returned the favour.'

'Pardon?'

'You returned the favour. Whatever she planned to

121

do you worked things out so that there always had to be a big English involvement. Not a nice way to treat a sweet old anglophobic lady.'

'She was no lady. My mother's a lady. That old hag was a harpie, an embittered old spinster. She had boiling bile for blood.'

'Very colourful.'

'She seemed to think that all the world's problems had their roots in English history including the development and spread of all things nuclear. She believed this was a point absolutely critical to one's understanding of everything related to disarmament. She couldn't accept that even if it was true, which it obviously wasn't, it didn't matter at all.'

'This report that she read from, did she leave it with you?'

Mooney snorted, 'Naturally not.'

'And she read everything in it out to all the other peace camp members?'

Silence.

'You're straining my psychic powers here. Well?'

'No.'

'How d'you know?'

'She mentioned some things, privately. Oh, that woman really thought she was so god-awful clever.'

'What "things"?'

'Absolutely nothing whatsoever to do with you or Alan or the peace camp,' she said quickly.

'What?'

'Nothing remotely titillating, I assure you.'

'I can pick up armfuls of titillation in any newsagent. Just tell me what was in the report, will you?'

'I tell you it's completely irrelevant.'

'I decide what is and what's not relevant. Just tell me. Don't you trust me?'

She looked him straight in the eye, surprised. 'Absolutely not!'

Well, what can you say to that? Naylor raised his eyebrows and his glass, afforded a silent toast to the wall opposite and belted back his Highland spring. He pushed his way through the gathering crowd to the bar and bought a vodka and, as there was no Absolut, ice.

Let us begin again, he thought. 'What do you know about *Clawback?*'

'About what?'

'Never mind. Just tell me what secrets you shared with Lexie Beattie.'

'Secrets? I don't think you possibly understand us. We are totally against secrecy. We believe in open – '

'Right. Right.' Naylor held up his hands. 'Then what secrets were you trying to uncover that she was involved in. I mean, anything at all. Is the commander down there in Glen Douglas trying to buy nuclear powered ducks for his bath? Anything.'

She frowned and thought about it. 'There was the Nirex thing but that's all.'

'Nirex? Tell me more.'

'She had heard a whisper to the effect that Nirex are investigating the possibility of building a very large site for nuclear waste processing and disposal in Strathclyde. I'm quite interested in that kind of thing. I was involved in getting rid of a very similar plant at home some time ago. Personally I think they're trying to re-site it here.'

'Mmmm, that potato could have been uncomfortably

warm. And she was looking for evidence?'

'Quite.'

'And that's all you know?'

'Yes, apart from the fact that they've supposed to have already had some discussions with Kromar about it.'

There it was once more. Kromar playing the bad penny. But this did not ring true to Naylor. A multinational like Kromar would find this too small a concern to do something as drastic as putting SB Services into action against an old woman. No. Completely out of the question.

'They're supposed to be considering the old Clydeholm shipyard site between Port Glasgow and Greenock. Rumour has it the contract's worth in excess of a billion pounds.'

And then again perhaps not completely out of the question.

'But it is all just rumour? There haven't been any announcements.'

'Well, she appeared quite thoroughly convinced. She mentioned something about a mole letting her see some papers.'

'I take it you're still interested?'

She shrugged. 'A little. But not much. What I'm really into is beating the military at their own game, showing them that even with their poisonous thermonuclear toys they will never be able to dictate to us, bully us, trample all over our future.'

'Uh, right. Right.'

'My name is Naylor. I'm from Munro Kerr Meikle, your solicitors.'

The rain was flicked up and down South Street and

into his face by a gusting wind. Leaning into the security communications box by the door, he listened for a reply. A movement above made him look up. A closed-circuit tv camera, swivelling, lens rolling into close-up.

'Hello?' He said.

A voice grated from the box. 'What do you want, Mr Naylor?'

'I want to speak to what his name? The chairman.'

'The Colonel dines at his club at this time every evening, Mr Naylor. I suggest you contact him there.'

'Hey. Just a minute.'

'Leave now, Mr Naylor. We know exactly who you are. You would be wise to go before we decide to remove you.'

'And you would be wise to make yourselves available. It might be more than a little embarrassing for you. In the witness box!'

'Is that a threat?'

'Of course its a threat, you dumpling!'

'I'm now alerting our dog handlers to see you from our front door. Have you ever seen an angry Rotweiller up close? They kill more than just children, Mr Naylor.'

'Prick.'

Three large voddies inside him to ward away the creeping chill within, he parked the Nova in the wet street about a hundred yards from his flat. Hunched under the rain he ran round the corner into his least favourite but handiest and most frequented off-license. The woman the locals called Metal Morag was behind the counter. She had the kind of face that tore open the side of the Titanic, cold, sharp and very very hard. How was it, Naylor wondered that in times of catastrophic unemployment the streets could be full of capable pleasant people and dragons like Metal Morag always found work? He felt sure that the system was not supposed to function this way. Or was it just jungle law, survival of the roughest?

There was no queue. He approached the floor to ceiling wire mesh grill adorned with MANAGEMENT RESERVES RIGHT OF REFUSAL and NO CREDIT and IT IS OUR POLICY TO PROSECUTE IN ALL INSTANCES OF THEFT.

Welcome one welcome all.

'I'm not sure I should serve you.'

Shit, here we go. Naylor gave a big, theatrical sigh. 'Perhaps you would care to explain the problem?'

'Last time you were in your cheque bounced.'

'Huh?' One problem he had not so far encountered was the bank. Sure, he had a five grand overdraft but it was all being converted quite amicably to a loan.

Metal Morag went into the back shop. A man with a dog came in. He said to Naylor, 'Hey, that your car at the corner yonder?'

Feeling a tiny swell of pride Naylor casually smiled and said, 'As a matter of fact it is.'

Metal Morag appeared from the back with a cheque saying, 'Well, here it is and as you can see its practically illegible. You must have been drunk as a rat when ye wrote it.'

'Well,' said the man with the dog, 'there's a couple of hooligans making a right mess of it.'

'What!'

Naylor was pounding along through the rain screaming curses at them, two of them. Big lads, bikers.

They turned when they saw him and laughed as they ran off. As he reached the Nova he heard the boom of two bikes bellowing and moving away.

It was horrible. Paintwork scored on the bonnet, aerial torn away, white and green spray paint along the bonnet and one side.

For fully half a minute he bounced with pure fury on the pavement. The he leaned against the wall and breathed deep and hard, gulped. He needed the vodka more than ever. Those were no teenage louts. Those were men in their twenties, late twenties, and they weren't out letting off high spirits either. Bastards!

Five minutes later he was climbing the steps to his flat, the Absolut in a white plastic carrier bag together with litre carton of fruit juice for the exigencies of the morning. Some comic was trying to put the frighteners on him. He was fairly phobic about cars after the Hamburg bombing. This little episode was helping matters not one bit, he decided.

As he struggled to unearth his house keys from the lining of his suit jacket he realised the door was open.

His breath caught, pulse quickened. Suddenly shivering he lowered the fruit juice and bag and raised the Absolut bottle, gripped by the neck in his right hand. The bikers had been there to throw him off his stride. The real problem lay in the house. But who? SB Services?

Was he fit to take anybody on? Overweight and seriously out of shape? Maybe not but he would have a go at smashing a head on his way down.

The front door swung back quietly. The lobby was dark, a light shining from under the room door ahead. Maybe he had merely interrupted a burglar in the execution of his preferred calling? He turned the handle, pushed it and jumped through in a crouch shouting,

'Yaaaaaaaargh!'

Big Bill Nicholson was sitting in the armchair, unimpressed. He was wearing a dark tweed herringbone overcoat, damp across the shoulders, collar turned up, fingers of both hands steepled before him.

'What in the name of Christ are you doing here?'

'And where "in the name of Christ" have you been for the past two days? You are, I believe, still retained as an employee by Munro Kerr Meikle – or am I grossly misreading the nature of our relationship? There are those individuals who join a firm with the intention of ruining its prospects in a particular location so that they may set up in opposition precisely in the same area as soon as their weakened opposition is at its lowest. That would be just about par for you I think, Mr Naylor. Exactly what the hell are you up to?'

'And exactly "what the hell" are you up to? That is my bloody car down there that your heavy boys just messed up.'

'Forget your car, Naylor. Start worrying seriously about your job.'

'How did you get in?' Naylor walked to the kitchenette, placed the Absolut on the draining board, took down a tumbler and poured a generous measure.

'It was not easy persuading the Partners to take you on in the first place, you know. They favour chaps with family connections to the law, preferably to the firm ...'

'I think you could be looking at a breaking and entry charge. And let's not forget vandalism, eh?'

'The concept of a junior partner who was an Army

man with minimal experience of civil law and only academically acquainted with Scottish law was difficult, not made easier by your family background, nor by the fact that you left school at sixteen ...'

'Can it,' Naylor said and sat on the bed. 'You know and I know the reason I got that job. You wanted to show the MoD how useful this could be. Wanted a little pull in there? Maybe your influence was on the wane with your military masters? Maybe you just wanted to sook up a wee bit more, eh? And don't give me all this stuff about MKM taking me on out of the goodness of their hearts. Remember I left Glasgow University with a double first and that knocks the degrees you and everyone else in this firm got into a pisspot. Another thing, they make money out of the Dumbarton office. Christ knows we all work long enough hours, including Wee Bobby Turner whom I gather is your resident spy. I bring work home every damn night. We do everything ourselves, our own precognitions, our own fee accounting, the works. And for what? Well, it must be for the glory of working for MKM because all this Junior Salaried Partner bit is rubbish. We've got no real say in the running of the firm and our wages are hardly better than a qualified assistant's. All of which, Mr Nicholson, is to say this brilliant job you've been so gracious as to let me cling on to is a bloody joke!'

Nicholson leaned forward and growled, 'You will find, you stupid, stupid little man that positions in law are not exactly hanging from the trees waiting to be plucked!'

'I'll get one. Just don't you worry. Now get out of here.'

Nicholson laughed. It was a nasty laugh, smug and sadistic at the same time. He said, 'You really think that after this farce anyone, and I mean *anyone* in this country would trust you enough to employ you? If you manage to get Banks to change his plea and drop this case you might just stay on in the Dumbarton office as an assistant. If not you are out on your arse without so much as a practising certificate to keep you warm! I shall personally see to that with great pleasure, I assure you!' He stood and flicked a piece of imaginary fluff from his coat forearm.

Naylor said, 'Oh, and how'll you manage that? I haven't put one ethical foot wrong here. Your Law Society chums can't touch me. The only person looking at serious trouble is you. Now what if I slipped a few interesting stories to the press about your "other interests"?'

'You may have noticed that there have been a few minor changes in the law recently making it extremely difficult for the press to carry anything smacking of official secrets unless the editor in question is feeling particularly suicidal or has had official sanction to print. All your attempts to fan the flames of interest are likely to secure are a longish spell in a maximum security prison, Naylor. You did sign the Official Secrets Act, remember?'

'Oh no. No way. I'll take it the Aussies, the Yanks, the Jerries. This is a stoater of a story, you know. You're involvement with SB Services, the scum who really did kill her. That and the *Clawback* papers they were looking for. And the fact she knew all about Kromar's wee scheme to convert the Clydeholm shipyard site into an atomic waste processing and disposal complex. News media all over the planet'll gobble that lot up and bugger the Official Secrets Act.'

There was a pause. Naylor realised that he'd just played all his cards in one go. He stood there breathing deep shaky breaths.

Quietly Nicholson said, 'How very unfortunate. You have just confirmed my darkest suspicions. I had no idea there was such a conflict of interest here, Mr Naylor. As to your interest in the Law Society let me enlighten you on another matter. I've written to an old friend highly placed in that august body. Just an informal note of explanation. Pointing out that we sacked you not only for gross negligence but because you let slip in your cups the fact that you spy on the peace-camp for the MoD. Nice twist don't you think? I've said that I'll probably have concrete evidence of same in the near future.'

He stood, pulled his coat together and added, 'Do not try contacting the MoD. No one at Kentigern House wants to know you any longer.' He took a pair of dark leather gloves from a pocket and began pulling them on. 'You have made some very fine people in sensitive positions look extremely foolish.' He tidied the check woolen scarf at his throat.

'They're quite capable of doing that for themselves, I'm sure.'

'And before you think of blabbing to the first journalist who chances by, examine these and think again about how you never put an ethical foot wrong. Goodbye.'

He pulled a large brown envelope from inside his coat and tossed it on the floor. As Naylor bent for it Nicholson walked out the door. His steps echoed back up the stairwell.

They were five-by-eight colour prints, ten of them altogether. Naylor's first shiver of dread was supplanted immediately by puzzlement. These were not the much publicised pictures of the Maltings fiasco. In fact it took him a few seconds to register just what they were. Debs

Mooney kissing a strange man beside a river or something?

Then he recognised the strange man as himself. And he remembered the Special Branch car that had followed him to the Inverbeg Inn on Saturday. This was Debs embracing him on the Loch Lomond shoreline.

Naylor could immediately see the title rolling off the Kinning Park presses: LAWYER BONKS BANKS' GIRL.

He ran to the window and swung it open to shout at Nicholson and stopped. Nicholson was standing at the open passenger door of a large black Daimler talking to the two thugs in biker gear. All three looked up. Nicholson said something to them and climbed in closing the door. As the Daimler moved away the thugs started back up the street towards Naylor's vandalised Nova. One freed a longish heavy chain from round his waist.

'No,' Naylor yelled. 'Touch it again and I'll kill you!'

He raced for the door and ran leaping down the stairwell out into the rain glossed black street and on and on, breathless to the corner.

The windshield and all the windows were shattered, upholstery ripped, tyres ribbon slashed. Naylor leaned on it and began to cry.

Nine:Lento

HE CALLED IN SICK. After all he was sick, or rather sickened. So he just stayed in bed wearing his bunny monogrammed black Playboy dressing gown, a relic from the '70s which Naylor still imagined to be the height of macho elegance. The Nova corpsed outside, rain pouring in. And that thought finally provided him enough stimulus to make another couple of calls. He reported the incident and the bikers to the cops and had the car towed off. Then he straightened out the insurance. No-claims totally nuked!

Late in the afternoon the phone started haranguing him. Psychic overtones told him it was the office. Annie Burns maybe. Maybe Big Buggering Bill. Five times it went off finally just ringing and ringing. On the thirty first ring he rose and picked it off the wall. The other end had hung up. He dropped it, letting the receiver whack off the floor and bounce on its cord.

The Absolut bottle lay totalled on the kitchen floor. He toed it under the sink and opened the fridge. Plenty of Highland Spring and a pack of chilly sausage rolls. He stuck four in the microwave for a couple of minutes, put them on a plate and poured a pint mug full of the carbonated water then hauled the lot back to his pit, careful to spill nothing on his prized royal blue duvet.

He used the remote to flip between TV channels and wound up watching kids' programmes, cartoon characters zapping monsters with lightning bolts – handy things those lightning bolts – Then a hammering began on the front door.

Stuffing the last daud of sausage roll into his mouth he swung out of bed.

'Jesus. Christ. I thought you'd tried to kill yourself or something!' It was Paul Goldman. 'D'you never ever answer your bloody phone? I've been trying to get hold of you since they told me you took the day off.'

'Okay, okay – keep the head. Come in. Close the door.' He shuffled back to the television. 'I'm completely pissed off. I just want one day in bed watching the adventures of a vegetarian vampire duck. Understandable in the circumstances.'

'I take it you're getting in deeper by the minute?'

Naylor pressed the kill button on the remote and the set clicked into suspended animation. They walked through into the kitchen and Naylor put the kettle on. He said, 'It'll have to be Lapsong suchong. There is simply nothing else. Not so much as an Oxo cube.'

Paul sat at the table. He said, 'Tell me what happened, for God's sake!'

So Naylor outlined the adventures of the previous day from smacking Turner on the nose to the wrecking of the Nova. He rattled through it all quickly showing no emotion. Then he just sat and looked at the screwed tight expression on his friend's face.

Goldman removed his glasses and cleaned them

nervously on a hanky. He said, 'Look, you are up to your armpits here. First thing. I want an affadavit from you covering all of this. Second thing. You have to get out, Jackie. It's too heavy. I mean do you really think that these, what'd'you call them, SB Services are involved? This is not just threatening to your career. I have a feeling that there is a major element of physical danger as well. Get out.'

'My own feelings precisely, old man. And tell me just how the fuck I am supposed to do that?'

'You go down to Central Station and get on the first train for London. Soon as you hit Euston you do a vanishing act.'

'Oh, sure great wonderful, just stick my whole life down the lavvy. No thanks a lot. I knocked my damn pan in putting that Dumbarton office on its bloody feet. And now I'm supposed to do a runner? Drop everything? My flat, my car, the works, by the way? Just because the arseholes of the world have decided its time to crap on me? Well, let me tell you this, boy, they've got another think coming if they think for one minute they've scared me so – '

'Jackie, what if they decide they want to kill you?'

'Oh, don't talk soft. All I'm doing is defending a man in court. That's what I'm paid to do. No big deal. Alright Big Bill Nicholson has his own reasons, whatever they are. Kromar's Clydeholm reprocessing plant or that damn *Clawback* document. Christ knows and doubtless SB Services is in deep as well.'

'Uh huh,' Paul nodded and got to his feet. He was not tall but he could give a good impersonation of stature, which stood him in good stead before a jury. 'You do realise that's a totally fatal attitude? Its exactly the attitude that my parent's families adopted in Germany during the thirties. Know what happened to them?'

'Paul! I don't have time for the hobby horse right now. Okay? Right? The worst that's likely to happen to me, and growing likelier by the minute, is that I wind up disbarred and ruined. Maybe I'm wrong but I see the only way of avoiding this is by contracting a serious long-term illness, something which will keep me safely hospitalised for the next six months.'

'Tell Banks there's a conflict of interest.'

'He's not interested. He thinks he's got bigger problems. If I back away he's going to scream to the press I've been nobbled.'

'That's just nonsense. It'd be *sub-judicae*. The press would never touch it.'

'These days they'll touch anything to do with lawyers! Look at the Harper scandal, one of the biggest most powerful solicitors in Scotland dragged through the gutter by its very own press!'

'Then you'll just have to make a clean breast of it all in court.'

'How am I going to make that stand up? My star bloody witness'll never come near a courtroom. He's number one on the Special Branch wanted list for Christ's sake, Paul! Use your skull.'

'So what happens?'

'Tomorrow I go down the Sheriff Court, the full commital, and I take it from there.'

That morning there was a big Culture City bash going on in Glasgow Green. As Naylor came down the Sheriff Court steps he thought about it, about going over to see the inflatable multi-coloured pavilions, listen to some music puzzle at the banners insisting there was a Lot of Glasgowing On in 1990 ... Maybe just nip over for a half hour or so. There was also a chill wind and a spit of rain so he pulled the black Burberry round him and tucked in his scarf.

He was standing there like that, briefcase trapped between his legs when a big man with another big man standing beside him asked him if he was John Naylor, solicitor.

Naylor looked from one to the other, extras from a tough-guy movie he thought. There were also a fair number of people about not to mention cops just the other side of the doors up there. He'd scream the bit out if they tried to grab him, stuff him into the back of a big black car.

Feeling brave he nodded.

The other one put his hand inside his jacket and Naylor froze. This was actually turning into a tough-guy movie. He drew out a long amber envelope and offered it.

'Huh?'

'This is an official communication from Munro Kerr Meikle, your employers, Mr Naylor.' He thrust it into Naylor's hand and the two men turned and made their way down the steps. Two ex-cops gone private, Naylor decided.

He phoned Paul Goldman who told him to stay calm. He'd meet him after work in the Dumbuck. So Naylor took a Dalmuir via Yoker from Argyle Street and opened the envelope on the train. There was a matching amber page within. It explained that he was no longer employed by MKM, professional misconduct blah blah cheque enclosed for one month's salary in lieu blah blah and please have your desk cleared by 5 o'clock blah blah ...

CHAPTER NINE

This sent his heart pounding around his chest, up his throat. It was all coming apart now. Ever since he was a boy soldier there had been an employer, a roof over the world, a guarantee that the money would materialise at the end of the month. Not now. No, who would employ him now? Now the arse was known by all to be hanging out his trousers? Now the world was holding him swinging by the heels and everything was falling out his pockets.

Folding the page back into the envelope he pocketed it and looked at the cheque. His last MKM cheque. Seven hundred and thirty two pounds eighty-five pence. With this you could buy enough good booze to poison yourself in two days. Buy enough Polish vodka to drown in.

Well, Naylor decided, this is it. I'm just about as far down as I can go. I can sign on but there's no chance of a job for me ever if I can't pull my arse out the fire. That toerag Nicholson. Right on the Court steps. Doing in my car, kicking the shite out my life.

Got to fight back. Got to. That's the one thing to keep right in front of your eyes now, Jackie. That you shall do unto Nicholson as he has done unto you in fucking spades, man!

So how in the name of Christ do you set about starting up your own show anyway? Go to the bank? Hello, I've just been given my jotters, the Law Society's probably getting ready to gut me and I'd like a fifty grand loan to open up an office? No. Have to run some kind of scam, a holding operation. Some kind of three card trick to keep them guessing till this is settled.

What if they stitch me up and I land in Barlinnie? Good place to pick up the criminal clientele. Ha ha bloody ha.

And where hell was Debs Mooney this morning? All the others turned up and a few almost familiar faces from the Faslane camp. Police, ever mindful of the Culture City cosmetics Glasgow was engaged in, shepherded them from view.

At Scotstounhill and he watched a fat man get off with two wee girls, daughters. All smiles. Naylor's eyes bled envy and hate at the three of them as the train pulled away. Some people don't know they're born, right enough.

Anyway where the hell am I going first? Clydebank and the off-licence or Dumbarton and a last sally through the office? Clear the desk? Break a window?

'Ladies,' Naylor announced planting a purple and white Haddows carrier bag on the double desk the typists used. They eyed him warily, like dogs awaiting a kick. Annie Burns stood in the doorway to his own office. The phone was ringing. He liked the thought he would not have to bother answering it. 'Ladies this is a small token of esteem which may be used by yourselves to celebrate my departure this day under a cloud of some ordure from the gilt flaking portals of MKM. In other words I have been given the boot. Bye bye and enjoy a wee bevvy at my expense. And yes you may drink the three chilled cheeky bottles of Vouvray demi-sec in office hours.' He unloaded the three bottles of not-the-completely-cheapest sparkling wine and a quarter pound box of Milk Tray onto the desk, a little amazed at his largesse on this occasion.

Annie Burns said, 'Oh, Mister Naylor they huvny.'

'They have indeed, Mrs Burns. Could one of you be so good as to take this now empty plastic bag and fill it with whatever personal effects of mine you find in that room?'

CHAPTER NINE

'Jesus, what'll happen to us?' said one of the typists as the other took the bag and walked off.

'The only person to be sacked is me. Nothing to do with anybody else at all. Well, in this office anyway.'

Annie Burns said, 'That's no' what she means, Mr Naylor. See him?' She jerked her thumb in the direction of Bobby Turner's office. 'See the punters? They canny go him. If you're for the off God knows what'll happen here.'

A warm smugness overcame Naylor. He said, 'Well, there's no if about it. I'm – as they say in the movies – history, my dear. How is he, as a matter of interest?'

The typist giggled. 'He's wearing a big bandage over his nose like a war wound. We think its an improvement. He's a face like a bag a spanners.'

Annie Burns asked, 'What about your files?'

'My files?'

'Your work in progress, Mr Naylor. I mean aren't they, strictly speaking, your own clients?'

Naylor sighed. 'Aye, well maybe but I mean what am I going to do with them? I don't have an office. Where am I supposed to see them, in the café? What do I use for filing cabinets? For a phone? I mean I'm snookered.'

'Then get an office of your own. God knows, look at the eejits that's made a go of it. There's morons walking about out there with the lawyers gowns on and their own offices. And if they can you can by the way. You're twice as brainy as the lot of them. Am I no' right, Ina?'

The other typist agreed.

'Mmmmmm.' said Naylor taking the plastic bag with his coffee mug, yesterday's *Herald* and his office toothbrush. 'Those books're mine too. I'll pick them up when I'm wheeled again.'

Annie Burns said, 'You pay for the taxi and I'll take them out to yours and drop them off on my way home the night.'

'Good,' he said. 'Smashin' '

'Let's drive about a bit,' said Paul Goldman.

'Let's get arseholed,' said Naylor. Then, 'Oh Jesus. Bloody Annie Burns is dropping my books off in a taxi and I told her I'd pay.' He looked at the time. Ten to six. Too late.

'Pay her tomorrow, okay? Now, let's go for a wee spin. Fresh air. Clear your head. Come on.'

'I'm a moron.'

'Jackie. Come on.'

Paul half dragged him from the bar to his Maestro and shoved Naylor inside. He sat huffily in the front passenger seat. Paul had to fasten the safety belt and told him he was behaving like a baby. Naylor's pout deepened, the lower lip thrust out a further quarter inch.

'Where to then?'

'Gobi desert. Who gives a – '

The car shot forward with a growl, drowning Naylor's words.

'Well, back to mine then. I'll stick you in the attic bedroom tonight.'

Naylor had a sharp vision of the seven year old twin daughters and their mother giving him an iced vinegar welcome.

'The peace-camp. Take me up the peace-camp.'

'Is that wise?'

'Is it wise? Its where I want to go. That's what it is.'

'I just meant that the trial – '

'I know what you just meant. Now, just take me there. Please? Okay?'

'Okay sure fine okay. Change the subject. Story. Absolutely true. Central Station the beginning of last week. Monday or Tuesday, right? Anyway there's this completely harassed mother, you know big shopping bags and so on and this screaming kid. So she's lost the rag and she's skelping it about the legs and who waltzes past but this German couple. You know, loaded down with the Culture City bilge brochures. And the wife says to the woman, "In Germany we do not beat our children" and the wee woman, quick as a flash says, "Aye, well in Partick we don't gas our Jews." ' Paul let rip a scream of laughter.

Naylor gaped at him and shook his head, said, 'Y'know, Paul you've got a real problem there. Jee-zuz. Between that and the tri-centenary of the Battle of the Boyne. God, some year of Culture.'

Paul started the tape player. Tex Ritter began singing High Noon.

'Come on. We're not going to be listening to this? Seriously?'

Paul smiled blissfully, said in a rubbish American accent, 'Do bears crap in the woods?'

Naylor said, 'Does the Pope wear a big hat?'

Together: 'Does the Pope crap in the woods?'

So they vroomed up the north bank of the Clyde playing at cowboys.

'Now, really, you've got give me this. I'm dedicated. I get shafted first thing in the morning and here I am, nearly sober and back on the job.' He gave himself a wee smile.

'I always said you and Albert Schweitzer were

142

incredible human beings, Jackie.'

'Sod off.'

They hummed, sang Tex Ritter's greatest hits, swapped insults all the way. Eventually they came off the new lochside road and pulled up to the camp.

Naylor sighed frowned and looked around. 'Where is everybody?' He climbed out and walked over to the caravans. Paul stayed at the car, arms folded, leaning on the bonnet. Naylor knocked on a couple of doors and there was a voice from within. He said, 'It's John Naylor, the lawyer.'

A perplexed woman looked out, her name ... was ... Sally? Susan!

'Hello, Susan. Left holding the kids, eh?' Inside were the five kids that belonged to the camp. 'What's going on?'

She stepped down but kept the door open. 'Oh, Mr Naylor, I've been trying to phone you all day. They say you're not working at that office now, in Dumbarton?'

'No, I – I'm opening my own place, you see.'

'Well, they were all lifted this morning at the court.'

'Lifted? I thought the police were just moving them out of the way of any TV cameras.'

'They went down to Alan's appearance in court. They thought there'd be a lot of press there and they could get some publicity out of it. They had big banners and all sorts of gear. Well, they were arrested for breach right away it seems. Police car came by around lunch to tell me.'

'I'll see about getting them out.'

'Well, I couldn't contact you so I had to find another lawyer.'

'Shit, what a time to lose clients.'

'I'm sorry, Mr Naylor. I didn't know what to do.'

'It's alright.' Totally ungrateful bitch how many times have I put the boat out for you lot and this is the thanks I get pushed down the Swanee as soon as the first thing goes wrong never mind all I've done for you lot time and time again …

'But it'll just be for this once 'cause I know you're doing great stuff for Alan and you're having a lot of hassles for us and we are grateful.'

Well. Too right.

'Where's Debs? I didn't see her down there today?'

'Oh, she's off with those Germans. They arrived on Saturday.'

'Germans? What Germans?'

'Er, you know. The … you know the hang-gliding people?'

'Are you telling me she's off hang-gliding just now?'

'Well … yes.'

'Hang-gliding. What do you know?'

'Listen. She asked me to post some stuff but I've been stuck in here. Could you …?'

'Aye, no bother, Susan.'

On the road home he looked at the letters, open addresses but unstamped.

'Reading the client's personal mail? Disciplinary tribunal stuff, pal,' said Goldman.

Naylor ignored him. There was one letter in French (this girl's educated) for Canada. The other was a typed article for a peace movement magazine about the need for a pan-European push to get British troops out of Ulster.

'Are you just naturally nosey? That really annoys me. You reading a client's personal mail.'

'Take a jump. Look, she's a witness and there's dirty work at the bloody crossroads. Bet your life I'm reading her letters. I'm the one that's getting torn apart not you. I'm looking at everything and I'm going to find out what the hell is going on here.'

'Right.'

'There's something way off centre here. I mean if you were up for commital today d'you think Ruth'd be away on a hang-gliding holiday? Seriously?'

'Don't ask for a serious answer. If I was up for commital she'd be up for divorce.'

Paul dropped him off at the close, shouted something about the following day, screamed the Maestro through a one-eighty and zoomed away like a jet fighter on afterburners. For a hairy driver he attracted a remarkable zero in damage and police attention. God has his favourites right enough.

Naylor climbed the stairs. In front of his door was a pile of books, a desk diary and five big taped bundles of files. Jee-zuz, she'd shipped half the office, more than half. For about half a minute he looked at the bundles and frowned. What the hell was he going to do with this lot? Then he began to laugh. He could see Bobby Turner's face when he opened a filing cabinet tomorrow.

Ya beauty! Wonderful filleting job.

Annie Burns, I love you.

Ten:Accelerando

THERE WAS A PHONE CALL from a reporter on the *News of the World* who had come into possession of certain pictures showing Naylor and Debs Mooney at the lochside.

'I'm led to believe that this woman in these is the co-accused in the Lexie Beattie murder case and that you're representing both her and her husband.'

'The woman in those photographs is not an accused in any case of which I am aware nor is she, to my knowledge, married.'

'And what's your relationship with her, then, eh?'

'Professional'

'You mean she's a prostitute?'

'What!?'

'You just said she's a pro.'

Naylor wished all this was a Bogart movie so he could just go out and shoot holes in this character.

'She's a client.'

'Is this the usual way you deal with your female clients, Mr Naylor?'

'She was distressed and wanted comforting. I just

147

happened to be around when she burst into tears.'

'Haven't you just been fired by your employer?'

'Huh? Er, I'm opening my own office if that's what you mean.'

'No, that's not what I mean. I mean you've just been fired. Isn't that true?'

'The nature of my departure from Munro Kerr Meikle is a private matter between me and them.'

'Not according to MKM it's not. They say they fired you yesterday. They say there's shennanigans going on between you and this female. They say she's Banks' woman and that somehow you managed to get charges against her dropped but somehow the charges against Banks have stuck. So he's still in the pokey but she's free as a bird. Some bird too, eh, Mr Naylor? By the way, have you stopped bonking her now? Yes or no?'

'Er what? No! I mean, no I haven't been ...Hello?'

The reporter had hung up on his explosive 'No!' – a really good line for a quote. Yes or no to a loaded question. Oldest courtroom trick in the world and he'd fallen for it.

He replaced the receiver for a couple of seconds then snatched it up again. Who to call about slapping an interdict on the potentially offending newspaper. As he was about to dial there were a number of clicks and he heard a tinny but identifiable voice saying 'Some bird too, eh, Mr Naylor? By the way, have you stopped bonking her now? Yes or no?' followed by his 'Er what? No! I mean, no I haven't been ... Hello?'

Very gingerly he sat the treacherous handset back on its cradle.

Who? SB Services? Special Branch? MoD? Parties yet to be identified? Someone was running telephone surveillance on him, someone not very good at it. That let out the MoD but nobody else.

He took the phone apart in case there was a bug inside and then started on the living room. By noon he was satisifed it was clean. If there were bugs planted anywhere else they could stay. Only a moron would plant anywhere else. As for the phone, well he hadn't worked his backside off in Army Intelligence without finding out just how ineffective they could be especially when the subject knew the game backwards.

Lunch was a 'Lean Cuisine' Coq au Vin. While it struggled to life in his microwave he nipped round to the chippy for a 50p bag of chips to go with it and picked up a couple of tins of Newcastle Brown in the off-licence. First thing to do was call up all the people he knew that he could use for agency work. Without support there was no way he could handle all the business he'd had at MKM. Mind you the office earned nearly a hundred and twenty grand last year. Maybe he could make a go of this.

No way to trust MKM. They might not be over keen to pass on his number to callers, even the revered Strathclyde Constabulary. Still he could rely on Annie Burns and the other two girls in the Dumbarton office for a while anyway. That was a relief. Anything he could rely on was a relief.

The microwave pinged and he was wondering if he should bother to shave today. The phone again. The press again?

'Hello!' He said, flat, unfriendly.

'Mr Naylor, I've just told St Vincent Street that they can stuff their job. That if you're going I'm going with you!'

'Annie?'

CHAPTER TEN

'That wee bastard Turner, d'you know what he did? He complained to them that I'd given you his client files. His client files, mind you. Christ, you could fit his files in a hand bag. So on comes that other big pain in the arse, Nicholson. Lord high'n'mighty, y'know? Said I'd to report down there the morrow mornin'. Do they think this is the bloody Army or something? Oh, I telt him a few home bloody truths alright. Both of them. Too true I did.'

'Oh, Annie Burns.'

'I comin' out to yours. And you owe me for that taxi last night. I've got a portable typewriter at home. I'm bringin' it and some paper I knocked from the office. You'll have to clear a table. We need some place for the files too. See if you've got space in a chest of drawers. I'll pack them.'

'Listen. I don't have the kind of money to pay you. I'm not … an employer. I – '

'Oh, I'll soon get you earnin', don't you worry about that.'

'Annie, you've got a wee girl. You've got to feed her and – '

'I've a twelve year old boy and I was always telt you raised weans on good food and good example but the good example came first. I'll be out at yours before half two.' And she hung up.

He sat there and felt tears come to his eyes and did not enjoy the feeling. Roughly he cleared his throat and deliberately started thinking about Alan Banks and the phone tap and SB Services. He popped a can of Newcastle Brown. Lunch.

'Well, you must be making a bloody good job of it if they're all trying so hard to bump you off the case,' said

Alan Banks.

'The biggest bump'll come on Sunday when the *News of the World* prints those pictures and claims I'm involved with Debs.'

'What do they think that's going to get them?'

'For starters they think it'll get you to join in the bumping proceedings!'

'Why are they so desperate to get you away from me, though? I mean I could just as likely pick some other reasonably sympathetic lawyer who'd put his all into it. Y'know? Like that John Carroll geezer that did the campers yesterday. I heard he was really good, know what I mean?'

Naylor sighed. 'Oh yeah.'

Right now he didn't need to know how good the other lawyers were who were walking innocently and happily off with his clients.

'What is this thing your employers particularly have about you, Mr Naylor?'

Naylor shook his head and shrugged. 'I can't figure it either. Really, I can't.'

What Naylor really really hated about Barlinnie was the smell, a century of steamed vegetables gone stale in urine and desperation. You could hang about an hour before they let you see your client and you just had to sit there and wait just like the prisoners.

The thing that was difficult to figure was the mentality of the men who worked here from choice. Not just the odd flying visit like Naylor, but day in day out, every day of their lives. Men looking through bars, behind big thick walls. Men institutionalised, bled of some of their freedom and some of their reason. Cruel men. Kind men. Some stupid and some very smart. Men stuffed into the ready

151

crammed galleries of humanity in dream dungeon homeos-
tasis, brick slabs insulating them from the flux and flow of
life beyond Barlinnie life. Just like the prisoners.

'There's a witness.'

Banks' eyes narrowed. 'A witness? Not Debs?'

'No. Look, I didn't want to mention him before. He
might just swing it if I can get him into court. Its going to
be a problem.'

The big man leaned back, folded his hands behind
his head and looked at the ceiling for a minute.

'For Christ sake, don't get my hopes up like this,
Mr Naylor.'

'Look, I can't keep this from you. It wouldn't be
right. The guy's an ex-para like you.'

'What?'

'I know it seems weird. He was coming up to see
her that day. Saw some characters leaving the place. He
thinks they belonged to a private security firm called SB
Services. He – '

'It's that wee fucker Haggerty, isn't it?'

'Er, you know this person?'

'He's hated me since we served together. If he's
involved its for reasons totally his own. He has no interest
at all in my predicament. None. I guarantee it. Honest.
Really, I do know this man, Mr Naylor. Very very well. He
can not be trusted.'

'Maybe but for the time being he's all we've got.'

'Well, I don't want him involved in any capacity. If
Haggerty gets the slightest chance to put the boot into me
he'll jump at it.'

'That bad?'

'I caught him trying to start a communist cell in the

Regiment. Can you imagine anyone that thick? Start a communist cell in the Parachute Regiment? Got the book thrown at him. Told me he'd get me back for it one fine day.'

'And this could be it?'

'Well, its a big opportunity.'

'He said Lexie Beattie despised you, that he felt you were only tolerated because you belonged to the camp.'

'Well, he got that wrong. She always said that Liverpool was really an Irish rather than an English city. Oh we had our fall-outs. I used to tell her she'd sold out, abandoned her principles to some extent. But I liked the old soul. She was good crack. No, she and Debs were always uncomfortable. Debs used to get angry with me when I wanted to go off and talk with Lexie. Maybe she was jealous.'

'Jealous of an eighty year old woman?'

Banks shrugged. 'Who knows? The heart's a strange place, Mr Naylor. Last couple of times she drove me down there she refused to come up. Started referring to Lexie as "that Beattie bitch." '

'Has Debs been around recently?'

'Not for a couple of days. She's busy.'

'Hang-gliding?'

Banks frowned and looked at the walls of the incredibly small interview room.

'I'd rather not talk about that. Can we change the subject?'

'Change the subject? Oh, yes we can change the subject.' Naylor looked at his notebook and took out a pen ready to write some more. 'I've spoken with the police and gone over their version of the events. According to them you weren't saying terribly sweet things about Lexie Beattie in the pub. Why was that?'

A thunder cloud came up over Banks' brow. 'You're supposed to be on my side.'

'The prosecution's going to ask you these questions and I want the answers first.'

'Oh. Right, right …'

'Had you been arguing with her that afternoon?'

Banks squirmed his big body in the small chair. 'Well … yes we did have an argument. A bad argument in fact. When I left I was really pissed off.'

'Have you ever killed anyone?'

'What?'

'It's relevant. One question from the prosecution is all it takes. Believe me.'

'No. Never!'

Naylor bluffed a show of flipping absently through his notes. 'Really? Never? I think I have something here?'

'I didn't kill him. The inquest showed it was the fault of the medics. I was exonerated.'

'Why don't you tell me all about it?' Naylor started writing.

Banks swallowed. In this tiny room it was difficult to look anywhere but directly in front of you at the person opposite and Banks obviously wanted to look elsewhere.

After about half a minute Naylor looked up at him. 'Is there some kind of problem here?'

Banks shook his head. 'No,' he said. 'It was a big NATO exercise in Germany. There were contingents from all the countries – '

'When was this?'

'Uh, spring '88. Mid-April. Operation Storm Front.

Supposed to test our readiness particularly against Spetsnaz and local insurgents. Spetsnaz are like the Red Army's SAS. They – '

'I know what Spetsnaz are, Alan. Go on.'

'I was on Red Team leading a small squad into an American air base. It was unbelievable. Know how we went in? You wouldn't credit it – through the front bloody gates! They knew there was an exercise on. They were all tooled up with their high-tech shit waiting for some stealth fighter bombers or crap like that. We hi-jacked an ambulance and dubbed it up as one of their own. Put on a few USAF uniforms. Then we radioed that there was an autobahn crash with a few of their boys in it and they sends out this team of medics. Soon as they're at the faked up crash we take them out, no problem. Then we head back with all but one of their ambulances and our own which is stowed out with explosives and all sorts of neat gear, like mortars and SAMs, you name it. Waved right in through the front door. Then I sent a signal that started a small diversion. Few thunderflashes and tape recordings of gunfire going off around the perimeter. Kept them on their toes til we were set up proper. Then we just took out the tower. Hit the hangers. Mortared the runways. Their super-duper base was out of it in less than a minute.'

His eyes were dull like someone half dreaming.

'Who got killed?'

'Medic. Went crackers in the hospital 'cause we were disrupting his wonderful casualty ward. So I "shot" him. You know, pointed an unloaded gun and said "Bang you're dead" and he wouldn't go with it. Picked up the phone to complain, to call the MPs ... So I hit him. And he went down ...'

'But didn't get back up again?'

Banks was quiet for a second. 'That's just it. He didn't get up again.'

'But they said it was his fault?'

'No, they said the other medics should have responded faster.'

'Why didn't they?'

'I'd told them they were all dead and not to budge. Silly buggers just left him lying on the floor. Autopsy showed that if they'd acted there and then and not half an hour later he'd have lived.'

'But you were disciplined?'

'Reprimanded. An excess of zeal, they said. My actions had intimidated the other medics into non-action. In other words the guy died because I'd scared them all witless.'

'Hmmmmm.' Naylor chewed on his lower lip and thought about it. 'They'll unearth this. They'll drag it into court on the first day.'

'How? There was no Court Martial. They won't be able to – '

Naylor shook his head. 'No, Alan. Never assume they won't find out. Let's say you're up there in the witness box and they ask you if you killed someone in Germany in spring 1988. Right? You're kaput.'

'How could they ever find out, Mr Naylor?'

'How? They have the best part of three months to get the basics of their case together. And its not just one wee lawyer like me, working out of his flat with a phone and a typewriter and an unpaid secretary. Its a titanic bureaucracy with staggering resources, networks of contacts that lead everywhere, computer databases all over the world, officia and unoffical ties, old pals, government and police forces to do their checking up for them ... And so it goes, on and on. If its there and somebody knows about it they'll probably find it. Now they may not but can we take that risk?'

'Suppose not. But listen, surely they can't just drop something like that in front of the court? Isn't there something about how they can't attack my character?'

Naylor gave a small laugh. 'Absolutely. Hundred per cent correct. And when the prosecuting counsel happens to mention it he'll be rapped hard over the knuckles by the judge. Very very very naughty. But what the hell, the jury will have heard. They'll be instructed to disregard it of course. But they will have heard, won't they?'

'Oh. Er ... well, after the eighty days when they've got their stuff together for the case, surely you'll be able to find out if they know about the Storm Front thing?'

'That, Alan, would be regarded as very naughty. In fact it'd be a miracle if I caught sight of the Crown papers before the big day. There's not really the kind of cooperation between the defence and prosecution you might imagine. I'll see some things of course, like the forensics. But all that's going to tell us is that she was beaten to death. Not helpful. But what can we expect from the Crown's forensic reports?'

'But surely we can get reports of our own? Independent ones?'

'If she was beaten to death she was beaten to death is there a point to another pathologist going over the Crown's work?'

'So ... What is there?'

'There's a few possibilities. If we can show that there may have been other parties involved we can show that there could have been other motives for her death.'

'You mean we have no option but to bring in Haggerty?'

'If we can get SB Services into the witness box maybe we can change it.'

'How?'

'There's a couple of elements here. The first is a hush hush plan called *Clawback*. Heard of it?'

'No.' He shook his head.

'Well, pin back your ears ...'

Eleven:Vivace

ANNIE BURNS SAID, 'I've got news for you.'

He was stunned. He'd walked out at half nine this morning for Barlinnie and come back to a different flat. It was ... clean? Tidy? It actually smelled different. The windows were open. Two sets of curtains were down and piled with bedclothes in the middle of the hall.

'What is this?'

Annie Burns ushered him into the kitchen, peeling off pink rubber gloves. The fridge was open, defrosting. A stack of freezer meals stuck out the top of the rubbish bag.

'What is this!'

'Only eejits eat food ten days past it's sell-by date.'

He began rifiling through the rejects. 'There's a fortune in here. Nearly fifteen quids worth of grub.'

'Must be the dearest salmonella in Clydebank. Sit down, I've got news. I mean it, you better sit down.'

Naylor blinked and sat at a kitchen table. She poured him tea in a red white and blue Rangers FC mug. She said, 'You've to get out to Glen Douglas. You know up by Loch Lomond?'

'The peace camp?'

She shook her head. 'No. The big army place. You've to go up there this minute. Call Boulevard and get Harry. Seems your girlfriend's right in it this time.'

'My girlfriend? What the hell're you talking about?'

'Deborah Mooney.'

Naylor stood. 'What about her?'

'The army's holding her. She and some pals broke in last night.'

'My God. They broke into Glen Douglas? Are they mad?'

'Don't ask me. They flew in. Those hang-glider things.'

'Jee-zuz! I don't believe it. This is too much. I'm in court this afternoon.'

'Paul Goldman's covering. Don't worry its all arranged. Call Harry and get out there.'

He sighed heavily and rubbed his eyes. 'I need an hour in bed.'

'You need your arse kicked. If you don't phone Boulevard I will and I'm not kiddin'. I'm working here on tick. Remember? And like they say in the pictures, the meter's runnin'. Get goin'!'

This time he was recognised as he waited for clearance at the gate. A young woman reporter from BBC Scotland knocked at the window. Nice looking, dark curly hair, a friendly and pretty face. Naylor rolled the window down.

'You're the lawyer in the Lexie Beattie case, aren't you?'

A portable camera was zooming in on Naylor from above and behind her shoulder.

'This matter is unrelated. I do a great deal of work for the peace campers.'

'How many are being held inside?'

'I only know one of them is a client.'

'Can you tell us who, please?'

'Sorry.'

'Is it Deborah Mooney, the wife of the accused in the Lexie Beattie murder?'

'I'm afraid I can't discuss this.' Starting to roll the window back up.'

'Who's representing the Germans? Are there any other foreign nationals involved?'

A sentry waved Naylor in through the swinging gate.

'Germans?' said Harry easing the car forward to the cluster of buildings ahead. He grinned. 'They finally invaded? Eh?'

Naylor was ushered into an office and greeted by a young captain. Army Intelligence of course. A thin face with thin features and big dove grey eyes that needed smart thin rimmed glasses. Naylor thought, I used to be you, pal, a juvenile smartarse in uniform. Only you're not that smart. How many times you been in Ulster, two, three? Looking forward to your next stint? I just bet.

'Captain Naylor? Pleased to meet you.' He smiled and shook Naylor by the hand, his grip firm but polite. 'I'm Captain Ambrose. Please ...'

Naylor sat down in the indicated grey moulded plastic seat. He knew this kind of office. It was ubiquitous from Denver to Delhi, from Murmansk to Melbourne. The potted plant, the laminated year planner taped to the wall, the computer terminal, the buttony telephone, the stacked magazines, the books, the desktop family pics and the wall heater, a couple of framed certificates and a decor designed not to offend. This narrow intense man could be an account- ant, an estate agent in uniform. Ambrose half sat half leaned on the edge of his desk. He was holding a file in his hands, leafing through close-typed pages. Eventually he cleared his throat.

'All this is rather awkward,' he said. 'I've gone over your reports for the last year quite closely and there really is no indication that anything like this was in the wind.'

'Oh. I see. Right.' Naylor sat up and cleared his throat. 'Can I ask how old is your latest material in my file?'

'Let me see ... week past Saturday. We received it yesterday.'

'Uh-huh. A week past Saturday. Mmmmm. Well then ... I don't think its that they don't trust me. If you look at the reports closely you'll see I only gave – *give* observa- tions based on my impressions of what's going on. I never ask any direct questions about their policy or plans. That would be a dead give away.' He smiled professionally.

Did this character really believe Naylor was still quoted at the MoD? Interesting, but step carefully. Dis- courage any phone calls to Kentigern House. Make sure you don't blow it and this little misunderstanding could work in your favour. But only if you want back into the good books of the men in Whitehall.

'Hmmmm.' Ambrose stood and walked round the desk and sat in his swivel chair. 'And no-one mentioned anything about hang-gliding?'

'Well, Debs Mooney did refer to it en passant some days ago. I assumed that she was just thinking of taking a sports holiday in the Bavarian Alps or something.'

'So you didn't include that?'

'Even if I had you'd still be in this mess.'

'We're not in a mess, Naylor. We took some time to get our hands on them but – '

'How long?'

He shrugged. 'Caught the first couple ten minutes after they landed.'

'How many of them were there?'

'A dozen.'

'And how long till you caught the last?'

'Mmmm, forty minutes?'

'Now that's what I call lucky, Captain Ambrose.'

'Luck had nothing to do with it, old man. Standard security procedures. That's all.'

'Exactly what I mean. Lucky.'

'I don't think I follow …'

'Lucky this wasn't one of those closely observed and documented exercises, eh? Even luckier they weren't Spetsnaz, wouldn't you say?'

'That's neither here nor there frankly. There's a lot to be done. I want you to go talk with Mooney and the others. We have a room fully wired for the purpose. Particularly we want to know if there are any other anti-NATO operations like this planned. Evidently we're dealing with a pan-Euro movement in the making here.'

'There is my professional standing as an officer of the court to consider, Ambrose. Client confidentiality and – '

'Oh piss on the play acting, Naylor. We'll keep you bulletproof.'

'And what happens when I'm disbarred?'

'You know and I know that will never happen.'

'Oh?'

'Can hardly afford to have you compromised now you're getting to the meaty stuff, can we? Mooney is going places in the international peace movement. Banks too if you manage to pull him out of the craphouse before it blows up on him. This would hardly be the point in time to have them lose confidence in you. Would it? Obviously we'll be making sure you appear squeaky clean at all times.'

'Really?'

'Why should I need to? My God, man, you were in Intelligence. You know the score. You are one of us and we look after our own as best we can. Especially when they're paying off. Soon as I ran Mooney's name through the computer you popped up. Absolute godsend I must say.'

'Godsend. Right. Suppose I'd better see her then, don't you think?'

'This way.'

Ambrose had put together a surveillance unit. Two rooms linked by a locked door with a full length inset of one way mirror glass. Behind it were cameras. The room was riddled with hidden mikes. Ambrose was quietly excited by the set up, like a wee boy.

He went into great detail concerning the areas that should be explored; the numbers, identities, nationalities and roles of everyone involved, who's idea it was, who provided leadership, who organised, who coordinated, who provided funds, who provided the various types of necessary expertise, what was the group's political affiliation, individual affiliations and on and on and on.

'Mr Naylor,' she said calm as you like.

He hardly recognised her. Baggy chocolate overalls and a charcoal combat jacket. Boots. Face blacked up. But the thatch of yellow-white hair was a giveaway.

She was marched into the room by two very young squaddies who immediately absented themselves.

'High jinks then, Debs?'

'Over three thousand feet high at one point, Mr Naylor.' She laughed and he smiled. The room was some ten feet square and very brightly lit. Furnishings included a small table and two more of the plastic seats, a big blue glass McEwans Lager ashtray and an Isle of Arran photographic calender for 1989. There was a door in the wall to one side of them. A glass door, mirrored glass. They sat opposite each another. He looked casually around. The gesture was not lost.

She bent forward and barked in a theatrical whisper, 'Do you think there's enough light for their cameras?'

He frowned, 'Surely the question is are we speaking loud enough for the mikes?'

'But of course,' she boomed, projecting her voice. Enjoying ever minute. Full of melodrama. Full of herself.

'Debs the first thing I have to tell you is that I am no longer working for Munro Kerr Meikle. I was fired yesterday for refusing to either convince Alan to kick a plea or to abandon him to his fate if he insisted on pursuing his claim to innocence.'

A look of real concern appeared. 'You poor dear, that's ghastly for you.'

Then she realised there was a subtext, a subtext for the listeners beyond the door. He was telling them something as well as her. Naylor watched her expression change slowly. Like that disorienting effect in certain movies when the camera pulls away from someone but zooms slowly in to compensate. The person seems to stay still while the whole world round them shifts in depth.

She would work it out, smart girl like her. He was letting them know Jack Naylor no longer did what he was told. Nobody was giving him orders any more.

Not MKM. Not ... them, the MoD.

She was watching the world shift in depth.

He waited a minute until he felt confident she had taken the process as far as she could far enough to realise that there was probably some kind of association between Naylor and the men behind the glass. Then he said, 'I told Alan this morning. He still wants me to represent him. I also told him that the *News of the World* has pictures of you and I at Loch Lomond. That time when you were upset and we ... embraced. They'll probably appear on Sunday. It is not going to be much fun. I'm afraid my career in all its aspects is in something of a nosedive right now, Debs.'

She was cool now, quite composed. 'How long till they come through the door?'

'Not long. Long enough to make a phone call. Long enough to ask a couple of questions and recheck my current status. This time on their central computers.'

'Right.'

'Do you want me to continue representing you?'

She was sunk in thought for a few moments. Then she shook her head. 'I'm sorry. No.'

He felt hurt, almost breathless. He stood up. 'Okay.'

'I'm sorry, Jack. Really and truly. I just can't take that big a risk.'

He knocked on the door, the real door. A key rattled and it opened. 'Goodbye then.'

Ambrose didn't materialise. He was met by the two squaddies. They marched him straight outside. The rain was starting and there was no sign of Harry. They bundled him into a Land Rover.

'Just a minute, where's my taxi?'

'They sent it away, sir.'

'What! Who sent it away?'

One squaddie pointed towards the gate. There was a red striped white Strathclyde police car sitting at the gate with its blue lights flashing. 'Them there, sir.'

'Aw Christ.'

'Jack, you're well shot of her. That's my opinion,' said Flanagan as they approached Balloch, rain trailing veils across the shrouded loch. 'It's a blessing in disguise. You'll excuse the cliché. She was using you. Putting you into some very dangerous territory indeed. Lamb to the slaughter, old son.'

How had the two of them had reached the Glen so quickly? Helicopter? No. Not fast enough. Spaceship? Their psychic powers were also well above par. How did they know she'd given him the push? Or was that naive? Yes, it was naive. They probably knew before he left the room.

'Right,' said Naylor. 'Just to satisfy a little curiosity on my part. Captain Ambrose or whatever his name and rank really were ...'

'Well, you have to excuse young Ambrose. The wee charade back there was his bright idea. Give you the idea he thought you were still bona-fide. Let you think here's your big chance to sook back in with Whitehall. Naturally he knows you've been dropped, your security clearance scrubbed, that you've been compromised and nobody can trust you an inch.' Flanagan's voice was quiet, flat. Mr

167

matter-of-fact. 'He knows because we told him this morning. Told him his wee scam was a waste of time as well.'

'So you knew I'd be coming out here, eh? Soon as they phoned me. Very interesting, Flan.'

'No,' said Rose. 'As soon as we discovered Mooney was involved we knew you'd be comin' out here. That right, Inspector?'

Flanagan nodded. 'We don't know anything about your phone calls, Jack, because its not our turn to tap your phone this week.' He paused and then looked round at Naylor. 'That was a wee joke, by the way.'

'Really?'

Flanagan shrugged. 'Try not to lose your sense of humour, Jack. Things might be a wee bit tough but a sense of humour gives you some perspective, old son.'

'You boys should be on Opportunity Knocks. Missing your big chance.'

Rose shook his head and said, 'Playing you like a fiddle, Mr Naylor. You know the reason she chucked you? She thought you were trying to outsmart her and she figured you might just manage if you were good enough. A risk she couldn't take.'

'I have to tell you that to me this is all garbage. Doesn't mean anything.'

'She's using Banksie too,' added Flanagan.

'How? I mean how can she possibly be using us?'

'That big bubbly bit down at the lochside.' Rose chuckled. Or was it more of a snigger? 'All done for our benefit, for the cameras. Something perfectly innocent which she knew we could and ultimately would use some way or another. Evidence that we're out to smear her, blackmail her. Makes them all rally round her. Pulls the

168

focus in on her. *Cause célèbre*, eh? That's a smart lady, Mr Naylor.'

Flanagan said, 'A smart dangerous lady. Very dangerous.'

'Maybe I'm growing cynical but I have this strange feeling you two might just be feeding me a line. After all, those pics of yours just happened to wind up in my boss's hands. Wonder how that came about, eh?'

'Come on, Jack,' said Flanagan. 'You know the score. He was owed a couple of wee favours by the monkeys up the top of the tree. It's poker, old son. He gives us a card, we give him a card. We're all playing. Look at you. What kind of hand are you playing? We don't know how much you know. We don't know what your committments are in this game. See, since you left your old roost with the MoD and Munro Kerr Meikle you're running wild. A random factor. Out of control. Up for grabs. Everybody wants to pull your wee strings. Even us. The difference between us and them is we tell you up front.'

'You want to recruit me? I don't believe this.'

Flanagan said, 'Maybe if you were ready to believe things a bit more readily, life might make more sense? No? A wee bit of cynicism can be the miracle ingredient in cleaning up the mess one gets oneself into.'

'I think I'm definitely acquiring some cynicism, Flan.'

Rose said, 'Take your fancy bit.'

'Pardon?'

'The one that just bumped you. Mooney.'

'My fancy bit? Is that another wee joke?'

Rose went on, unheeding. 'Now a bit of cynicism there might have changed your view of things.'

169

'Like what?'

'Your telling me your MoD pals never cracked a light about her?'

'What do you mean my MoD pals?'

'We know the score between you and them, Mr Naylor. They bared their chest this morning.'

Naylor sighed.

Flanagan said, 'If its any consolation we sympathise. They live in toyland, Jack. Its a bit different out on the real streets.'

Rose said, 'For my money Debs Mooney is Provisional IRA and has been for the past five years.'

Naylor shook his head. 'Look. I do not believe this. Whatever fairytale you're going to spin, I'm just not going to believe it. That's the ground rules. Long as you know you can them go ahead. Say your bit.'

'Just listen to the man,' Rose said. 'A little education can go a long long way.'

Flanagan said, 'Well, I'll tell you the way we see it. Is that fair? In 1983 she was at St Annie's College, Oxford reading history and politics. She frequented the debates and spoke up on Irish issues. Her old man is a don. A world expert on Rennaissance music. He's Irish, born of an old Cork protestant family that have been up to their ears in Republican politics since the days of Wolf Tone. I mean these are people with fanatacism in their genes. Right?'

'If you say so.'

'She met up with a young Belfast man also at Oxford. He recruited her. He was killed in a wee contretemps with the Army in the Armagh bandit country. That was 1987. Round about the same time she joined the Green Party and CND. She moved up here and started writing for the peace movement mags and the press on dismarmament and green issues. You know the kind of thing.'

'So? What's the tie in, Flan?'

'This same smart lady has convinced the upper echelons of the Provos that they should put pressure on the peace movements to kick the British Army out of Northern Ireland. The Home Office and the Northern Ireland Office take this quite seriously. There was only a loose association amongst the peace groups in Europe. They were rarely involved in what you might call joint manoeuvres. And when they were nobody took much notice. Well, we knew she was up to something but this takes the top prize. Blue ribbon stuff.'

'Just 'cause there's a few Jerries in there with her?'

Flanagan smiled. 'I told you she was a smart lady. She specialises in recruiting ex-army types. All your "Jerries" belonged until recently to the West German Armed Forces. And up there on the mountain they launched from − a wee satellite uplink station and a couple of engineers.'

'Eh?'

'They went in with night-adapted TV cameras and transmission packs. The whole episode went live to a German network. They put it down on videotape and phoned up the news brokers. It was on breakfast TV all over Europe this morning. Except Britain. Aparently the picture quality is not up acceptable standards.' He chuckled. 'The news story's just breaking here. There was a report on the lunchtime news.'

Naylor raised his eyebrows. 'Have to admit, though. Bloody impressive.'

'The international organisation she needs doesn't

exist. Yet. So the smart lady is putting it together with her own two hands. When its completed she'll be at the top.'

'So you want me to pal up to her. Is that it? Want me to suck in? You want someone keeping close tabs on her. Someone to report back what's going on?' Naylor shook his head. 'I'm out of that business now. Anyway, if you people have been so concerned about her antics you should have planted someone on her long before now.'

Rose snorted in disbelief. 'Well, of course somebody was planted on her. Wasn't he? Not by us. Probably by our masters. I mean they don't tell us everything.'

Naylor swallowed. 'Oh God.'

Alan Banks.

Rose said, 'But now that particular gentleman is no longer in the picture. In fact he's likely to be out of it for a very long time. The smart lady's quite safe. Very convenient for her. Wouldn't you say?'

Flanagan nodded. 'Welcome to the chase, old son. Just that sometimes its not easy telling the hunter from the hunted.'

Twelve:Capriccioso

'IT USED TO BE A CHIP SHOP but it went on fire, by the way. They think the guy did an insureandburn on it so they're no' paying up.'

'Uh?'

Naylor was deep in the Friday morning press. He'd wakened feeling completely unfamiliar with himself. No hangover and a particularly good night's sleep. Wellbeing, that's what it was. It lasted until he picked up the papers with the bread and milk from the corner shop. The *News of the World* had been unable to hold the story.

The *Sun* had it.

LEGAL LOVE NEST splattered across the front page with a big pic of himself and Debs Mooney kissing. Her face was carefully fudged and no details of the case were given. Just that Naylor was making free with the girlfriend of a client locked up and awaiting trial on an extremely serious charge. And there was a rumour that the Law Society was about to make moves of some undisclosed nature. He felt sick. Bought an extra quart of milk and a packet of Rennies.

'It's in Birgidale Road. We'll get it for a song. Guy's

desperate for the money. And my cousin Betty knows a fella in the City Chambers. Nice fella. He's something to do with planning permissions and things like that.'

The phone went again. Again Annie Burns answered and told the *Sunday Mail,* this time, that Mr Naylor was still not back from court. She wasn't expecting him until around 5 o'clock that afternoon. Thank you.

'Uch. One thing I canny go its self-pity.' She strode across the kitchen and snapped the *Sun* from his grasp and shoved it into the rubbish bin.'

'Just one damn minute!' Naylor shouted.

She stuck a foot in the bin and mashed the paper deep inside.

His chest heaved. Blood pressure rocketed. 'I'm sick to death of being shoved around. Do this do that do the next thing. Nobody kicks me around any more. Get this straight. I am not a fucking dog! I am a fully grown adult male. And let me tell you, lady, let me tell you – ' standing and hammering his forefinger onto the kitchen table – 'as from this minute you take your orders from me and not the other way round. I don't give a damn that your'e working here on tick. Either you work here or you don't. That's your choice. But if you work here you better get it through your head that I run things not you! I say what's to be done and when and where this goes and that goes, and …'

She was standing looking at him with her arms folded and tapping her foot, a skinny sharp featured Glasgow woman in her early thirties, brown hair frosting fast to grey, brown eyes that hard they could cut glass and a mouth always twisted down at one corner.

'Right,' she said. She picked up the phone and dropped the receiver in front of him. 'Now you've done me, start on somebody it'll do some good with. Nicholson. The Law Society. The *Sun*. You want to kick back, well three cheers for you but you better be able to kick more than a wee seven stone Partick woman, mister. Or you're finished!' She pulled a padded purple anorak from the back of a chair and shoved her arms into the sleeves. 'Now, I'm going down to Safeway to get some messages for you and me. I've taken a tenner out your wallet. By the time I get back which'll be in about an hour we'll be ready to eat and you'll have fired a few rockets up their bums. That a deal?' She wheeled a tartan shooper out from a cupboard.

Naylor nodded. 'Aye, fine.' And he sighed, picked up the phone and drummed in MKM's number. 'Being right all the time must be a great burden, Annie.'

'Well, its like anything else, Mr Naylor, ye just have to learn to live wi' it. Oh, and by the by, your garage people phoned. Your motor's good as new and you can pick it up this afternoon.'

He caught a smirk on her face as she pulled the front door behind her.

The Nova was back. The sun was peeking through the proverbial clouds. The pearl diver had surfaced from the depths and how sweet was the cool fresh air. Take a lungful and roar.

She was right too. He phoned Nicholson and shouted at him. Told him unless MKM climbed off his back he was going to the Law Society with a complaint against the firm. They had blabbed to the *Sun* about his leaving them. Disgraceful unprofessional behaviour. And while he was at it he'd tell them how Big Bill passed the photos along from Special Branch to Kinning Park. Furthermore there was a good chance the press would hear about his complaints. They seemed to have such great sources, didn't they? Then he told him the new Secrets Act could go stuff itself. He had figured out how to do it. How to get television coverage and everything. He was ready to mail shot every MP with full details of Nicholson's antics and MKM's involvement. There would be questions in the House within forty-eight hours. So up yours Big Bill. Ha ha ha.

Mmmm, yeah, now that felt nice.

Law Society next. Good afternoon, I'm the latest Scottish solicitor to be lambasted in the press. Don't you think this state of affairs is becoming a trifle ridiculous? Why does the Society not try a new tack, just for a change? What about publicly denouncing of this kind of press behaviour? Why instead do you cower away, say nothing, hide? Or, if the target is sufficiently small and defenceless, join in the attack, yourselves? What's up? No Bottle? Not fit to stand up and defend your members? Maybe its time for a nice juicy "Outsider" piece in the *Glasgow Herald* on just how shoddy your record really is? Hmmm?

Then he phoned Paul Goldman. Paul, sue the *Sun* for ... five hundred grand. No, make it a million. Don't argue. Do it. Please? And find out if they're to be done for contempt of court. This must have a bearing on the case. Right? Oh and another minor detail ... I'm wheeled again! Yaaaaay! Get the Nova this afternoon. I'll call you back about tonight. I fancy a classic Blitz session.

Yes, that did feel good. Oh yes. Really really good.

Naylor stood, stretched and walked over to the fridge. Adequate supplies but no Absolut inside. Ah well, pick some up later. He didn't really need it, not now. Now he could readily face the big bad world again. He had to go to Barlinnie to see a client this afternoon. When he was there he'd ask to see Banks too.

He could face him now as well.

'I feel I should give up talking to you and just punch your lights out.'

'Well, I wouldn't advise it, Mr Naylor. I'm a big lad and I'm trained for the job. You're not. No offence intended.'

'You heard about Debs and the hang-gliding drop into Glen Douglas?'

He shrugged. 'I even helped organise it. Had a lot of ex-army contacts here and in Germany. The hang-gliding was her idea, so was the televising bit. That was the real jewel in the old crown, you know. It's the publicity that really hurts, causes the real screaming and shouting. I mean look at the Faslane campers. They're in and out of that base all the time. Can get into the damn nuclear subs and everything but to make an impact you need national television coverage. That's the secret and that's what we got. International television coverage. The best.'

'Does she know about you?'

'What in particular?'

'F branch in particular.'

Banks stared at him blankly. 'You mean MI5?'

'No. Oh no. The girl guides. Jesus. "You mean MI5". Stork margarine wouldn't melt in your mouth, right enough, Banksie.'

'Seriously? You think I'm MI5?'

'Ah, now we're getting somewhere. So she doesn't know. Or at least we think she doesn't know. Chances are however that she does. In fact I'd go so far as to say I'm certain she's absolutely one hundred percent sure you are an F branch plant. The evidence is overwhelming.'

'What are you going on about, Mr Naylor?'

'She had Lexie Beattie killed to incriminate you, my friend. To get you out of her hair. You were too close, knew too much about her plans.'

'That's just totally crazy, Mr Naylor. Everyone in the camp knew about the drop on Glen Douglas.'

'And do they all know she's a member of the Provisional IRA with a remit to form a pan-Euro peace organisation that'll pressurise Whitehall to pull the Brits out of Ulster? Eh?'

'Oh ... Well. If you say so,' shaking his head.

'No only you know that. You were planted on her. Your people knew she was looking for ex-servicemen to join the ranks of the peace movement. Right? And an ex-para officer must have been tempting, eh? Too tempting to resist?'

The big man looked more and more depressed. 'Mr Naylor, who's been telling you all these nonsense stories about me?'

'Special Branch.'

Banks laughed. 'Special Branch? Oh, that's all right then. I was worried there for a couple of jiffs. You don't really believe a word they say. Do you?'

'Well ...'

'Mind you it is funny them saying that about Debs and Northern Ireland. I remember there was something a while ago.'

'Like what?'

'Now let me see. It was, what, maybe eighteen months ago. Yes, about March or April last year. She was over seeing the family of an old student friend of hers who died. I think he was killed in the troubles. Can't remember the details. Anyway she came back with this story about how the Provos had stopped a big nuclear waste reprocessing plant being built there. Now why did she mention that? Oh, yes. She was slagging the record of the Northern Ireland Office on the environment. She's a Green you know.'

'I know.'

'Right. Anyway I says something like, well maybe they're bad but I'm sure the Provos are hardly better. Right?'

Naylor shrugged.

'Oh, not at all she says. Their record's one of the best, and then she goes on about this island off the Antrim coast. What's it's name? You know, the one the locals say Robert the Bruce went to when he saw that daft spider in the cave?'

Naylor frowned. He'd always assumed the spider event to have taken place somewhere fairly local but with exotic overtones, like Rutherglen or Wishaw.

Banks snapped his fingers. It sounded like a firecracker. 'Rathlin Island.' He beamed at Naylor. 'Now, what were they up to?'

'Who?'

'That's what I'm trying to remember. Heard of a company called Kromar?'

Naylor squeezed his eyes shut like he was awaiting a blow. 'What about them?'

'It's coming back to me. Really.' The big man smiled broadly. 'They had this plan with Nirex, the nuclear reprocessing people to build some big nuclear reprocessing plant off-shore and they were thinking of Rathlin.'

'A Kromar and Nirex plan for a nuclear waste

reprocessing facility.' This was depressingly familiar. 'And what transpired?'

'Well, Debs said that the Provos blocked it, frightened them off. It seems they demanded an exorbitant cash sum, several millions, before they would allow them to build it. Got too hot for the parties involved and they took off for pastures green.'

'Did Debs ever mention this to Lexie Beattie?'

'No, I – Oh, just a minute. You know, I think you're right. I think I remember them talking about that or something similar.'

'And does the name "Clydeholm" mean anything to you?'

'About as much as bubblededub means to you.'

'Uh huh, be that as it may. I think we're going to try putting Miss Mooney in the witness box.'

'Debs? All she can say is she dropped me off, she picked me up and went to Asda in between.'

'Well, perhaps we can question her about her IRA connections and how they tie into this case.'

'Dear me, the old Special Branch's certainly done a number on you and no mistake. Look, Mr Naylor, I don't want Debs dragged into this. I love her, you know. She loves me back. She didn't have Lexie Beattie killed. I don't know what schemes the Branch is weaving you into but believe me, that's all they are. Just policemen trying to manipulate you.'

'And I suppose you and Mooney aren't?'

'Well, no, we're not trying to manipulate you.'

'Like hell you're not. Everybody's trying to manipulate me. And I want Mooney on the witness stand answering questions about her position in the Provos and whether or not it compromises her position in the peace movement. Answering questions about whether or not she knew the mandarins in Whitehall had sent you up north to keep and eye on her. And did she subsequently discover what you were and kill Lexie Beattie for something to pin on you and have you sent by-byes for a few years?'

'No, you can't do that. No.'

'Really? And here was me thinking I could do much as I damned well liked.'

'Well. I suppose there's two things, Mr Naylor. Two ways of looking at it. Lets assume that you're right on everything and I'm MI5 and she's IRA – '

'Provos.'

'Provos, then. Well, if that's the case I'd not want my position in the peace movement compromised, would I? If I get off I'd like to be able to go back and resume my spy work from where I left off. And there's the second point. Assume that neither of us is involved with spies or the IRA or anything like that. Assume that we're just a couple of peace campers in trouble and that we happen to love one another. All of which is true. Do you really think I want that destroyed by you putting her in the witness box and making a lot of slimy suggestions about spying and the IRA to make it look like she did it and that her big drive for a pan-Euro movement is nothing but a sham front for the Provos? That would demolish us. Demolish me. Demolish her and all she's struggled to put together ever since her Irish boyfriend was killed. Putting her on the witness stand would be an act of wanton social vandalism.'

'It may come to that,' said Naylor but doubt was proliferating in his mind once more.

Banks pushed his chin forward and said, 'It won't

come to that, believe me. I'll sack you as my solicitor before it comes to that.' He leaned forward, his expression changing, hardening. 'And remember all those nasty tales I can spin about how you always told me everything to say every time I went to court? I'll shout that out til my lungs rupture! Be careful where my woman is concerned, Mr Naylor.'

Naylor was playing Mendelssohn's violin concerto full belt on the cassette deck as he raced down the Dumbarton Road. The Dumbuck and Paul Goldman beckoned. Paul promised some juicy tales about exactly how the News International lawyers had responded to the writ for defamation.

Naylor was giggling too much, dum deedeeing too much.

Annie Burns had told him she'd been in discussion with the fellow who leased the burned out Castlemilk chip shop. He'd agreed to rent it out if Naylor could afford a decent cash advance and guarantee to lease it for a minimum of two years. Annie had hummed and hawed the money down to a blinding three and a half grand a year, six months in advance. They'd have to decorate the place themselves. No problem. Annie knew a woman in Scotstoun whose man was a gaffer with Havelocks.

Naylor had felt like scooping her up in his arms and kissing her madly and passionately except he suspected he'd have received that sharp boned knee in his tender places for his troubles. He laughed. Naylor and Co. was up and running.

It would still cost a few bob and the big wrestling match with the bank still lay ahead but he knew Paul was going to come through tonight. Paul the golden man was going to tell him something nice had been arranged regarding the finances, at least pro tem.

Naylor was grinning too much, laughing too much.

Naylor was paying too little attention to the rear view mirror.

It was a rented van, bright red with AVIS on the side and it had pulled out of Caledonia Street the moment he went past and stuck right behind him, cutting up a wee black Escort in the process. A few cars honked it but the red van ignored everything but sticking right up behind Naylor.

The lights went red at the bottom of Mountblow Rd and Naylor cruised to a stop. The van cut out into the oncoming traffic. Drivers screamed and bellowed. Lights flashed. Horns sounded. Naylor frowned and looked round.

There was a big side door being thrown back and two men leaping out.

'Christ!' He let out the handbrake but too late the door was open, the safety belt cut and he was being dragged out. Got in a knucklepunch to the groin of one and he went down and Naylor pulled free again and dived back into the car, slammed into gear and drove across the traffic stream, door swinging open into an oncoming car. Bang. Door gone.

The red van screamed up on the inside and whammed him almost into a big double decker. He swerved, the Nova's tail lashing off the bus. Then they hit him from behind and went back to the inside. Where were they? Both wing mirrors were gone. The inside one showed his left knee and the gear stick.

Slammed again. this time he swerved between two small saloons and was screeching up Old Dalnottar Road the van overtaking on the inside and swerving right and

Naylor hit the brakes but not fast enough and he was into the back of an ice-cream van. Naylor cursed and tried to find reverse. He found it as an iron bar exploded through the window.

Blackout ...

There was pain and nausea. He was on a floor and the floor was moving. He cracked and eye slightly open and saw three men crouched by him. Donkey jackets, jeans and very dirty faces under woollen caps.

Play dead or at least unconscious. Jee-zuz, my drawers ... oh no. The smell amused them. They nudged each other and sniggered.

The journey seemed endless. It grew dark outside. The van was twisting here and there, round and down, this way, that. Naylor had no concept of where they might be. Why take me all this way if they're going to kill me? Because they're going to torture me first. Maybe they want to know what I know about ... what? Who the hell were they anyway? SB Services? The IRA? Official harassment from the corridors of power?

It stopped and the side doors opened. It was dark and cold and they threw him to the ground.

'Now, Mr Naylor, either you tell us where Haggerty is or we kick shit out of you. Then we'll leave you in that trough of pig slurry over there. Tomorrow you're going to start behaving yourself.'

Thirteen:Adagio

NAYLOR BEHAVED HIMSELF for weeks. The Scottish papers went on a lawyer trashing binge focused on himself with the only consolation a promise from a senior editor on the *Glasgow Herald* that if he wanted to reply they'd make space for him in their pages. It wasn't much of a consolation.

He'd still wake up at night screaming for them to stop hurting him, long after the broken fingers, the broken nose and the cracked ribs had healed, after the twenty-three stitches were removed from his face, long after the last of the massive bruises had turned yellow and faded.

He always woke and hour or two too early. Depression waited there like a fog for his opening his eyes, a fog of dull pain and self-loathing.

He'd lie there without moving. Looking at the flock wall paper and trying not to think. There were different tricks like trying to remember some episode from a tele soap he'd watched the previous night. Remember every detail of the camera movement and the script, how the actors had handled their parts. Or there was a mantra. A word he'd just keep repeating in his head until the alarm went off and he would get up and go on automatic pilot. Years ago he'd talked with a man who 'debriefed' suspected IRA members in Belfast. He said that everyone breaks, just some go quicker than others. Once they're smashed they never get it back. Well, sometimes but the circumstances had to be exceptional.

There was nothing exceptional about Naylor and he knew it. He knew he was not even a very good lawyer, never had been, never likely to be. He was pushy and cantankerous. Anyway his aspirations had nothing to do with being better at his job. Why should they? He looked at his peers and saw the hard workers, the skilled practitioners and it seemed to him that their chances of worldly success were no better than the dullards, the buffoons and the monkeys. Advocates weren't smarter than solicitors. He'd once thought this had to be so. No more were High Court judges sharper than a good sheriff. It was the luck of the draw. Everybody had his moments of brilliance but some were noted and others ignored. The trick was to get noted and be quoted. Join a political party like the Tories, as he had done. Join the masons, as he'd been trying to do. That was how it worked. Go to all the professional functions and be nice to the right people. Crawl a bit. Suck up a bit. That was the game. Or so he had thought. Now he was out of play. Now he just watched and waited and strung along.

The poison Nicholson had dropped in the correct ear finally did its work. The Law Society were after his blood for spying on the peace-camp. They wanted him on the carpet early in December. He imagined them lining up in their dozens to be picked for his tribunal. Rubbing their hands, licking their greasy lips. Jackals at the feast. But he could not hate them. His fire was out. His belly gone cold.

He became a sober and quiet recluse. Out to the office in the morning, punctual, opening the doors at half eight. The smell of the burned fat, ghosts of pie suppers were still there haunting the background but he seemed to be doing all right. Business was coming in. Annie Burns and a typist handled the running of the office.

Perversely, the press publicity had actually brought clients through the door. Morbid curiosity, he supposed. Lots of sad grey women with marital problems. He wondered what kind of solutions they expected from him. A weekend in Brodick with some sexual solace?

And then the old wheels began turning. Naylor grew into their lives like a tree, became part of them and their problems, the pathetic drunks, the addicts, the shoplifters and the random assaults. There was enough left of his heart to tick over. Annie Burns kept slipping the odd brown note on his request to women whose men were doing time or had been abandoned with weans. Sometimes she'd just go out to the Oxfam and buy up clothes for them. Dish them out as and when. That was her way. Then she'd tell him off for "putting the boat out all the time and who cares?" He didn't even think about it.

Meanwhile there was Melanie Forbes becoming Mrs Francis Lambie. A big piece in the *Milngavie and Bearsden Herald*. A spread of pictures. She looked sensational in the wedding dress. But his jealousy was lukewarm, almost without passion.

Lambie had sent Naylor an invite to the wedding. Naylor kept it in the top drawer of his desk. He wanted to tear it up but he was afraid. He was afraid of everything.

At night he would watch television and videos and wait for the phone to ring. It always rang. There was always someone at the other end but not always the same person. They always asked if Jackie had been a good boy today. Had Haggerty paid a visit? Then they would give a little laugh and hang up. One evening he was watching an opera on the box and he took the phone off the hook. And they phoned him in the office the next day and told him that if it happened again he'd get more smackies and Jackie didn't like getting smackies. Did he?

Annie Burns did not like the new Naylor but she understood the change and what caused it. Her language was clipped and sharp and her manner disapproving, saying I didn't dig you out of that hole for you to dig yourself another. She hated self pity but she seemed to suss that his was more than just that.

Paul Goldman was always on the phone or at the flat, mollycoddling him, worrying about him, arranging the criminal injuries compensation. There were no more Blitz nights, only the occasional visit to the opera. But even *The Trojans* drove Naylor out of the Theatre Royal. The culture snob in him was barely alive. Cinema was his best bet. He and Paul would go once a week. Nothing violent; they'd gone to see Mike Douglas' *Black Rain* and Naylor started vomiting near the end. On Fridays they took a carry out curry from the Shish Mahal back to Naylor's flat. They drank a little, some wine or beer but not much. Paul told him he had to talk it all over with the police. Maybe phone up Pitt Street and talk to Flan again. But see somebody. This, he pointed out, was classic terrorism. Nazism. Controlling people by terrifying them. And what was Naylor doing about the Beattie affair?

Nothing.

A defence counsel stepped forward as if primed,

probably was primed. Collared Naylor one day on the High Court steps. Naylor was using him to handle another murder case. Abused housewife pours boiling chip pan over brutal, drunk and unconscious husband and then sets him alight; man wakes screaming in front of his two scared weans and jumps through window, twelve stories up a tower block.

The advocate was mediocre, known to have a fondness for Edinburgh club life, claret and rent boys. A call left on his answering machine was returned within hours which made Naylor suspect that this man was not exactly overburdened with work. Not that Naylor cared. Even when he came out with it quite bluntly ...

Instructed counsel for the Lexie Beattie thing then, Jack?

No, how about you?

Well, I just might fit it in. Now, let's take a look at my diary ...

He saw Banks and told him about it all. Said he wouldn't be calling SB Services to the stand. Wouldn't involve Debs Mooney. Maybe Banks should get another lawyer after all because the defence was non-existent. Banks was sanguine about it, sympathetic. Well, an unknown person called the police, he said. We know that was Haggerty. We'll just have to use him as the lynchpin, Mr Naylor. Doesn't look like I've any option.

Eight weeks had passed without a whisper from Haggerty. Even Hasties detective agency had drawn a blank. The APG's front man seemed to have evaporated like a small summer puddle in strong sunlight.

He was to be the sole defence now. There had been a call to the Cranstonhill police station, his call. All there, clearly documented, members of the jury. Someone went into Lexie Beattie's flat after Banks had left. Banks said that when he left her she was alive. This person raised the alarm, said she was dead. Have the police produced this individual? So we have a person unaccounted for and yet the police insist that the accused was responsible. Yes, he visited Lexie Beattie that day. Yes, they had an argument. All this is admitted. But was his behaviour really that of a man who has just murdered? Did he try to flee, fake an alibi or cover his tracks? No he went straight to the nearest hostelry after a very public argument with the very person who could have whisked him rapidly away from the scene of the crime.

Naylor play-acted it out time and time again. He contacted counsel and went over it all with him. The advocate said the best they could hope for was a verdict of not proven. He thought that it probably wise not to belabour the missing witness bit. After all, the police claimed that the voice on the phone was muffled. In their opinion it was Banks himself. A fit of conscience. That kind of thing. He was probably going down anyway and it might be nice to try getting on the good side of the bench. Make as few waves as possible and hope that you'll thus attract a not too punitive sentence.

Time was Naylor would have sacked counsel for suggesting anything like this. Not now. He took it. He swallowed it. He nodded agreement. Probably best thing to do in the circumstances.

Just that there was something else not quite right and it worried like a ragged nail. He felt he should know more, should be at least convinced of Banks' innocence. Once upon a time he had been, before that police car ride back from Glen Douglas. Alan Banks. His whole attitude to this was too glib. So cool so calm. The floor caving in and the walls are falling down around his ears and this character's cool as you like. The only reason he'd act that way would be if he were hiding something. But what was he hiding? Why was he so sure of Debs Mooney? Why was he so willing to go to prison? Unless he knew for some reason that he was not going there? But how? What? And was he really MI5? And if he is why has no one come out and pulled him clear of the flak? No none of it added up now. It was a morass, a sucking swamp. Nothing seemed solid any longer.

And then he would reprimand himself. Thinking like that leads to trouble and pain. It leads to the farmyard and the four men in donkey jackets and the tub of liquid pigshit. It leads to them tearing your clothes off and pissing on them. Hammering you with their steel toecapped boots and pickaxe handles and making you beg for more through your smashed mouth.

Then the others look on and cheer and laugh and joke and drink lager while one of them sodomises you, rapes you.

Whenever that memory returns he fights it. It is the only time he fights now. It revolts him so thoroughly, so deeply, he bites his hand hard for the pain to make it go away, to put his mental equipment back on line and into gear. He never considered rape, certainly never from a victim's point of view, nobody ever told him it was like a burglary, someone breaking into your body and clawing out your soul. Leaving flesh and mind all mixed together in a bloody mess.

There were deep breathing exercises he'd read in a Yoga book of Ruth Goldman's Paul brought over. They could help when it got to him badly. But nothing could make it go away all the way.

All that mattered was coming out of all this alive. That would the victory, the only victory. Paul had explained it was like living in a concentration camp. There were ways of dealing with it. Techniques for staying alive. Thousands of people had done it before. Dachau, Buchenwald, Auschwitz. Survivors. Hemmed in by violence all round. Death keeking through the curtains. Keep your head down. And you are one of the lucky ones.

Lying in bed staring at the dark ceiling Naylor would reassure himself. There are people like Annie Burns and Paul Goldman who'll always always be there for you, to help you, protect you, give you comfort and pick you up when you fall, wipe your nose. Somebody loves you. You have to get through this for them, Jackie, not just yourself ...

Come though it alive. That's all anybody asks. In these days, in this city, its enough to breathe, to walk free and unmolested; its enough to be a survivor.

Three days before the trial all that changed with a bang.

One of the sad women was in his office. She sat opposite, her proto-psychotic eleven year old son standing staring out the back window at a brick wall and dustbins. Sometimes she wanted Naylor to stop her husband from visiting, visits consisted of kicking the door down and kicking her and the boy black and blue. They were supposedly separated. But when her man was sober he was all regrets and she could never follow through. Interdicts don't hold up when you tell him he can bring up his laundry or have a watch of the telly while you cook him the odd meal. Last night she had finally called the cops. Called them after the man took a knife to her. The injuries were superficial but he also had a go at the cops. Bad bad move. He was up on an assault charge at Glasgow Sheriff Court that afternoon. She was a Crown witness. Today she wanted Naylor to 'get the charges dropped.' Like too many of the television courtroom educated she assumed that the charges could just be dropped. She didn't grasp the point Naylor kept repeating; that this was not a matter for herself or him or the police. It was in the hands of the procurator fiscal and there was no chance of it being dropped. Not the proverbial snowball's in hell.

Phone. Naylor picked it up.

'Yes?'

'There's a man on won't give his name. I don't think its those funny people again. D'you want to take it?'

'Right, er, okay, Annie,' He closed his eyes, braced himself.

It was a familiar surprising voice. 'Been hearin' you've had a wee bit o bother, pal.'

Haggerty.

'Who's speaking, please?'

'I'd to kinda hot foot it out the country for a while there. Know what I mean and that? Wasny there when you needed me, eh? Look, I think we should huv a blether. I've some stuff I want to hand you. Hot stuff.'

'I don't want or need anything from you, Haggerty. You hear?'

'Er, thought you wanted me to do the witness bit? Changed your mind? I'll be in touch.'

'No, I – ' but he'd rung off.

He hit a switch on the phone. 'Annie, I need a big mug of strong black coffee, two spoonfuls.'

'That stuff's murder.' Annie had seen a programme about coffee and become an expert.

'Please.'

He ushered the woman with the locked up husband out into the street and told her to go to court and be quiet. Tried to explain that shouting at the bench was contempt of court. Knew the next time he saw her she'd probably be locked up and boy in care somewhere.

'Annie, get me Paul Goldman.'

'What's up? You look helluva peely-wally.'

'Is there anyone else in the diary for this morning?'

'You've to make a few phone calls. That's all. But there's a big bundle of fee notes to get through. You should get an assistant, and I'm no' kidding.'

Naylor said, 'A qualified assistant? They come in at twelve, thirteen grand a year these days. And why bother when I'm out of business this time next month? There's three other law offices in Castlemilk to look after the interest of the local denizens. They don't need me.'

'Naw, but I need ye and she needs ye,' indicating the typist with a jab of her thumb. 'And our weans need ye. So you're going to come through that tribunal wi' flyin' colours. I hope that's clear?'

Turning to the typist he said, 'If bottle was all you needed, Annie Burns would be ruling the world by now. Can I get a couple of cocodamol with that coffee?'

He sat down with the fee notes and went to pick up a pen. His hands were shaking. Carefully he gripped the sides of the desk lightly and began a slow intake of breath measuring it into his stomach by the cool long inch. And then slowly slowly out. They'll know about Haggerty. Slowly in. Think about the breathing. concentrate on the sensation of air being carefully inhaled and expelled. They'll tell me to be a good boy and then they'll mention Haggerty. Or maybe they'll be waiting for me at home …

'Here's yer coffee and co— My God, Mr Naylor you'll have to see a doctor about this. Here hold on I'll get a wet cloth and the sponge.'

He'd missed the fee notes but the mess was only part in the waste bin, the rest had hit the carpet and his shoes. He was still retching when she came back on the run. She had two damp cloths, one for his face.

'Here. You poor soul. Its no' fair.'

Taking Paul's advice he decided to close up early. Go out to Rhu and stay low for a couple of days. Paul's partners would let him look after Naylor's Castlemilk operation for a week or so after the murder trial. They didn't approve. Paul didn't give a damn.

The back of three o'clock the last client was out the door and he turned the sign to Closed. Annie and the typist were ready to go in seconds.

'Give you ladies a lift?'

'Brilliant.' said Annie. The typist agreed. He usually gave Annie a run home but they typist liked to get away sharp as she had to pay a babysitter for the extra hour that she had to work after her wee girl came back from school.

'Right.' He tossed the car keys to Annie. 'You two go ahead. I'll get my coat.'

The two women ran out, pulling their coats about them in the wind and rain. Annie opened the door and folded down the driver's seat and got into the back since the typist would be getting out first. She leaned over and opened the front passenger door. The other woman climbed in, closed the door, stretched across and closed the driver's door.

The explosion blew in the glass front of the office. Naylor would certainly have been shredded had he not been in his own room pulling on his Burberry. The shockwave tore off the door and slammed him against the wall. There was smoke. Dazed, coughing and bleeding he scrambled to his feet, staggered into the street dimly aware of a familiarity. For a few moments he thought he was back in Hamburg. But how could it be Hamburg in Castlemilk? There was wreckage scattered everywhere. Broken windows and the remains of the Nova lying twenty feet away on its back, a fire smearing up from the underside.

Further up the street a woman started screaming, then another.

Fourteen:Fortississimo

'Colonel, I'm so pleased to meet you.'

The emaciated man with the steel wool moustache looked up from his dinner.

'Pardon, do I know you?'

Naylor pulled back a seat and planked himself down opposite the thin grey man with the watery blue eyes.

'Not by sight, sir. Your boys have been running a number on me for months so you'll know the name. Naylor. Jack Naylor.'

He stopped chewing and his mouth opened ever so slightly.

Naylor went on, raising his voice. 'Sorry about the bomb thingy, old man. 'Fraid your chaps messed it up. Got my secretary and a typist by mistake. Damn shame all things considered.'

Other club members in the dining room were looking round, looking at each other.

'Get out of here before I have you thrown out!' the little man growled his face reddening.

'That is precisely what I am hoping for, colonel. Outside there, in Blythswood Square are a number of reporters and photographers. They just love me. I'm their meat and drink. Remember? And when your stewards throw me out I'm going to tell them I was here accusing the chairman of SB Services of murder, of bombing my car. They'll be waiting for you next, wanting some piccies of you coming out, wanting your quotes on the matter. Tell you something else. Most of them love people like you about as much as they love people like me.'

The red face was freezing. Two uniformed stewards were approaching. He waved them away.

'Think this is bad? Think again, old man. Know what I did after they told me I'd one woman dead and another in a coma? Nothing. Just nothing. I just stood there and it all happened, like a change in the weather, snow falling. People like you you don't know it but there's another army out there, an army in the streets, in them rows and rows and rows of tin tenements that go on of for fucking ever. An army of what you and everybody else calls the scum. After the cops had done with me and the ambulances and fire brigade were gone two men came up to me. Two dealers. You have heard of dealers? No, I mean street dealers, not the big timers you run protection for. I mean the ones that get dirty and do time for you and your pals. The ones your clients suck in by upping the price so high the only way they can get the stuff is by dealing it on the streets themselves!'

He banged the table and the cutlery and plates jumped. A coffee cup tumbled to the carpet. The stewards were still being held back by the colonel's frantic waving.

Naylor heard a whisper behind, someone saying *call the police this is serious*. Oh nice one. Get the cops to arrest you and whisk you away from the club, magic you past the press. Nice one, but it's not going to happen.

'I've swung a few good results for them and one or two of their friends. So I talked to them. I told them all about it. Everything. Even how your trained monkeys battered the shite out of me. And raped me. Terrorised me. They said I should have come to them. Know something? They were dead right.' His voice dropped to a dry whisper that the thin man could only just hear. 'So then I started thinking about all the heavy guys I've done favours for in the past. Y'now, slipping the wife and weans the odd tenner when the man's doing time? Bringing a packet of Embassy up to Barlinnie? Not to mention always turning up for them at some police station in the middle of the night in the rain when they've been bust. Maybe you find this difficult to believe but they actually remember things like that. They experience that bizarre feeling we call gratitude of which I'm certain you've probably heard rumours. Well now they're going to return the favour, Colonel. If I say so, or if anything happens to me they're going to return that very special favour of this afternoon to you personally. Very personally.'

Naylor stood, picked a small boiled potato from the Colonel's plate and popped it in his mouth. Then he reached across, took the fork from the man's slack right hand and shook it.

He smiled. 'Welcome to hell, Colonel.'

There was a large trolley loaded with deserts by the entrance to the dining room. Hands in pockets Naylor walked towards the doors. He winked at a big steward, lifted his leg and toed a bowl of trifle upending it on the carpet. The man lunged at him, another grabbing him in a half nelson from behind and they began running him up the stairs. Distantly Naylor could hear voices protesting. No no

– the police –

Too late. He was outside, being tossed down the steps before a delighted gaggle of pressmen. He'd lie to them, say he was thrown out because he accused the Colonel of murder. Good Story. Cameras flashed. 'Mr Naylor. Mr Naylor.'

Now the reporters all knew him.

Man of mystery no longer.

'Is she going to live, doctor?'

'She's sustained an incredible amount of damage, Mr Naylor. She's also undergone three major operations since she came in here this afternoon. Including the amputation of both legs above the knee. On top of all that she's in a coma. If I told you I thought she was going to live more than another few hours I'd be a liar. In fact I suspect the only reason she didn't die immediately is she was in the back of the car and the bomb was under the driver's seat from what I gather.'

'Right.'

They wouldn't let him in to see her. Apparently they only let you into Intensive Care if you were next of kin or something similar and even then they were fussy.

Naylor walked into the waiting area. There was a big beetroot faced woman with short glossy black hair and dressed in a smart black raincoat. A fair haired teenager in a school uniform sat reading a Batman comic beside her. Or maybe not quite a teenager. He looked up at Naylor as he sat down and Naylor saw Annie Burns staring out of his face.

He rummaged frantically for the name.

'Er ... David? I'm John Naylor. Your mother works

for me.'

The boy just continued to look at him.

'I'm Annie's sister-in-law, Mr Naylor.' The woman said. 'Geraldine Burns.' She leaned forward and offered her hand. He rose a couple of inches off his seat, shook it and sank back. David, he realised was not so much looking at him as through him. She nudged him. 'David, this is Mr Naylor, your mum's boss. Say hello.'

The boy's eyes shifted focus. 'Oh,' he said. 'Oh hello, Mr Naylor. Is my mum still alive?'

Very well spoken, very proper and polite, very well turned out. Jesus Christ what have I done to you?

'Well …' What do you say? What can you say? 'Well, I was talking with one of the doctors there just now and he said she's had some operations and she's resting. She doesn't seem to be getting any worse just now.'

'She's in a coma?'

'He, er, he mentioned something about that. Yes.'

'You read a lot in the papers about people coming out of comas after being in them for years. Don't you?'

'Uh-huh. I've read stories like that. Now and then.'

'They give you a false picture. The majority of coma patients survive less than thirty six hours. Did you know that?'

'Er …'

The big woman said, 'Oh don't be so morbid, David. Your mother's going to be perfectly all right.'

'No she's not. She's had her legs cut off. She's definitely not going to be all right, Auntie Gerry.'

'Read your comic, David.'

'It's a graphic novel. Adults read them too. Have you ever read a graphic novel, Mr Naylor?'

'Um. Can't say I have, son.'

'This one's all about how Batman comes back to Gotham City after he's been retired for ten years. It's one of the best graphic novels ever written.'

Get me Batman right now. I could do with him.

'I brought in my mum's favourite tape too but they don't have a player so I'll have to bring one in tomorrow. They say they'll let her hear it. She can have it on my Walkman. I've got an adaptor unit that plugs into the mains so there's no worry about the batteries running down.'

'What tape's that, then David?'

'It's the one by that woman that sings "Power of Love". Mum plays it all the time at home. She sings it to me.'

The doors parted and Paul Goldman walked in.

'Thought I might find you here. How is she Jackie?'

'Dare I say as well as can be expected in the circumstances?'

Paul sat down. He said, 'It'll take more than a firecracker to kill Annie Burns,' and put his arm round Naylor's shoulders.

Haggerty had found a place in Possil that suited him. It had been a supermarket. Now it was closed. Roll blind metal shutters permanently down and decorated with abusive graffiti. He found a way in by forcing a few bars off one window at the rear. They could be pulled back into place easily. From within you could unbolt the back doors, cheapskates had taken the padlocks with them. This allowed him to roll his bike safely inside.

Not that his secret was really safe from the multitude of kids who played around and ran through the courts. But that never bothered Haggerty so long as he was safe from the police he was safe, period. Or so he believed.

He had a small Calor gas fire blazing away and his tranny tuned to a Country & Western programme on BBC Radio Scotland. The remains of a black pudding supper had been scooped into a paper ball and projected into the outer darkness of the shop's interior.

The fire was bright enough to read by and he was leaning back against the wheel of the Kawasaki, leafing through the pages of his favourite work of literature, *A Disaffection* by James Kelman. It was a big well-used hardback in a plastic cover which he'd liberated from the shelves of Stirling's Public Library. He'd actually played snooker with the author years before and still could not quite get over the fact that he knew somebody who'd been short listed for the Booker prize. Not that he was really sure what the prize was but he knew it was impressive. And that was enough.

Crunch of a foot tread.

'Feel free to come an' join us.' He spun round, back to the wall, kicked the gas fire so that it turned to face the intruders and pulled a knife from his jacket. It's evil nine-inch-long blade glittered in the gas light.

Two half bricks bounced off his chest. He cried out and dropped the knife. 'Jesus,' he gasped. 'Mammydaddy. Oh. Mammydaddy.'

Figures moved closer and something held before them came sharply into focus. Two tubes, metal tubes, stuck together? The twin barrels of a shotgun.

'Well, we meet again, Mr Haggerty, but on my terms this time.'

'Mr Naylor?'

'Smart boy.' Naylor moved into the light and stood looking down at him. Turning his head to indicate the shadowy figures beyond he said. 'The Angels. Fine upstanding members of their chosen calling, Mr Haggerty. Good and loyal friends of mine as well. Thought you could hide out in the streets away from all the eyes? Not their eyes, you can't. They put the word round that they're looking for somebody in this city and they find them. I know you're quite proud that your friends are so well connected. Well, the Angels're my connection now. In the words of the song, there's nobody does it better.'

'Hah.' Haggerty sat up, rubbing his chest. 'Gives a whole new kind of depth to the phrase "criminal lawyer", eh? What're you after?'

'I want you to tell me what the hell is going on. I want to know exactly what this bloody runaround game is all about. Just over eight hours ago my car was blown up. A woman that works for me was killed, another's in a coma. People in the shops and houses round about were torn up with flying glass. How come this happens the day you phone me up?'

'Jesus. Look will you take yon bloody popgun out ma face?'

Naylor turned, clicked the safety on and arced the shotgun back into the dark. Somebody caught it and clicked the safety off again.

Haggerty said. 'Are you gonny shoot me, pal?'

'Only if you lie. Then we'll give this place some redecorating and you'll be the paint, Haggerty.'

'Point taken, you know? What do you want me to talk about?'

'Oh. I'm sure you can dig up something to entertain

me this evening. Let's get comfy.' So saying he pulled over a plastic milk crate, upended it and sat down. 'Come on, Haggerty!'

Haggerty looked off to where the others stood, barely visible. How many were there? Three? There was the soft metallic sound of the shotgun hammers being drawn back.

So Haggerty explained ...

In the wake of 1987 General Election the Ministry of Defence commissioned a study on the limitation and containment of damage to the rest of the United Kingdom and the Western Alliance should Scotland's politicians declare for unilateral independence and reconvene the Scottish Parliament. The study was farmed out to Heriot Watt University and to a private consultancy, SB Services, the latter gathering and collating all relevant data and supplying the input of military expertise. Analysis and political assessments were undertaken by the academics involved. It was intended that the Study Group should provide updated assessments between 1988 and 1992 at six monthly intervals.

The *Clawback* Study Group reported first in the summer of '88. The government circulated a few confidential copies of the work to certain carefully selected senior civil servants and individuals in the private sector. This move was principally concerned with retaining confidence that the Government, although hugely misrepresenting the political aspirations of the people of Scotland, could still retain effective control of that country in a political crisis for a period sufficient to permit a satisfactory realisation of assets or their re-siting elsewhere in the UK or abroad. Loss of life would be restricted to the low hundreds and restricted almost entirely to the ethnic population.

The Study Group report received a very positive response, particularly from individuals highly placed in the CBI who saw their elected government standing up for their interests.

Where it did not go down well was amongst those few Scots industrialists and financiers who caught a glimpse of it. Here they saw an insidious set up. The government of their choice was prepared to take such actions in the event of a UDI as would drive any subsequent Scottish government unacceptably far to the left and sever the important trade and financial arteries with the south.

There was no forum for discussion, so no opinion from the Scottish business community could be considered. Nor was such input sought. Business men and bankers perturbed by these events considered the options open to them. There was no point in taking it to the press. That would only precipitate an outcry again likely to throw Scotland left politically and closer to nationalism. No one in Whitehall would admit to the official existence of the Study Group report so it was useless to keep pursuing that avenue.

Ultimately it was decided that the best course of action would be to compromise the credibility of the Study Group members and so call into question the report's validity. There was little point trying to discredit the academics: to do so would have required recruiting other academics. SB Services on the other hand was a business and that they all understood.

They reasoned that a security services company like this one could be seriously discredited if some of the dirty tricks operations it ran were made public and scandal ensued. That they ran such operations which would not concern the masters and the mandarins. Their concern would centre on the fact that the company were sloppy enough to have allowed the cat out of the bag. Such sloppiness would indicate a serious lapse of professionalism and immediately call into question the value of their contribution to the Study Group. Their own security would be a serious matter of doubt and the Study Group Report would have to be suppressed if not actually scrapped.

The consequences for SB Services would hurt twice over. First they would lose their annual six figure income from the Study Group. Secondly, more important, their image would be fatally soiled. They would no longer be regarded as solid, substantial, really dependable and professional. News of their bungling ineptitude would spread and those quietly powerful people in all the right places would conveniently lose one's telephone number.

Soon one would be totally edited from the favour of the upper echelon. Then, as the word trickled down, one would very rapidly become simply a hack operation, strictly small time and very strictly low income.

'So what did these business men and bankers do, Haggerty? Hire you?'

'Naw. I showed them it, pal. I was the one who opened their eyes in the first place, so to speak.'

'And how did you get it?'

'Oh dolly dimple. I used to work for them. Didn't I? Haaaww, that got you! Right? Full a wee surprises, eh? I was one of SB Services' top honchos, man.'

'Even though you were slung out the paras for trying to organise a communist cell?'

'Well, telt them it was yer youthful indiscretion an'

that, know whit a mean? What, I said, politics? Me? These days? You've got to be jokin', pal, I said. Ach they lapped it up stinkin'. Know what they did? Wait'll I tell you. It's a killer. It's a real killer.'

He was warming to the story, enthusiasm bubbling in his voice, 'They taught us a' these "dirty tricks techniques", like how to break into places an' bug them an' get into their safes an' their computers. Kinda Stow College for industrial espionage an' that. Follow me? Right. So know what I did? I did it right back on them. Used everything they'd taught us on yon courses and cleaned them out. An' I mean right out. Zapped all their computer disks. I mean I got printouts first. Right? I'm no' that stupid. I mean they'd a' this stuff copied aff the MI5 Registry. Goldmine. Then I opened all their filin' cabinets when I was finished an' sprinkled them wi' whisky an' set them on fire. See you use whisky so that the fire brigade boys that check up tell the insurance that their was whisky involved and they think it was a drunken manager or somethin'. Ages before they stump up the insurance. S'that no' brilliant, man? Eh?'

'You posted copies to a carefully selected handful of the most interested parties in the Scottish business community. Why didn't you just give it straight to the Scot Nats? They'd've gone public like a shot.'

'Exactly. Wee bit of the premature ejaculations. Tend to get overexcited. So what would've happened? They'd've gone mental. Screamin' their lungs out in public. By now yer political capital on *Clawback* 'd be tuppence. Naw, it's got to break in the run up to the next election or its nothin'. An' frankly there's too many jessies in the SNP for me.'

'So who'll break it? Scottish Workers' Republican Party?'

'Aye, somebody like that.'

'Meanwhile you cream a nice wee profit from your bankers and business men by keeping it hushed up and sticking SB Services up to their oxters in it.'

'The APG's got to get the ol' foldin' greenbacks some way or other. Right?'

'You never went up to her flat that day, did you, Haggerty? You never saw her there. And you never saw any bloody SB Services people there either. Did you?'

Haggerty's expression changed. Fear opened in his face.

'You set me up, you little bastard!' Naylor screamed, backhanded him hard across the face. 'You knew what they'd do. You knew they'd bug me, tap my phones, everything. Christ, you even knew SB bloody Services would be listening in when you called me this morning. Right? They thought you were going to give me some crap that would totally crucify them. Right? That's why they put the bomb on the car. Isn't it! Isn't it!'

Haggerty's eyes looked round wildly. Suddenly the shotgun muzzle was pinning his chest to the wall.

Haggerty started sweating.

His breathing was harsh and low. 'But I can make up for it, honest. Just gimme a wee chance, Mr Naylor. Please?'

'How are you going to make it up?' Naylor shouted. 'How? You dirty little man? Tell the dead woman's wee girl your going to make it up. Tell the woman with no legs who's probably going to die tonight? How d'you make it up to her, her family? How? You! Moronic! Maggot! How!?'

CHAPTER FOURTEEN

Then Naylor smelled something sickeningly familiar. He looked again at the cowering weeping heap before him and he thought, its happening to me, I'm becoming one of them ...

'Mr Naylor,' he sobbed. 'Please, don't kill me. No' yet. Its no' time. No' here like this. Naaaw. Aw naaw-www ...'

'Okay.' said Naylor. 'Okay.' And the gunman backed off.

He drew in a shaking breath. 'You said on the phone you'd something hot for me. Well, you better have. Want to live? Get me it! Get me everything you can lay your filthy hands on! Everything!'

Fifteen:Sforzando

A SPLENDID ETHEREAL voice sang "The Power of Love" over and over again in the intensive care unit. Naylor could hear it in the waiting area. At first it gave him gooseflesh but eventually he grew used to the uncannily pure tones. Gradually it just became musical wallpaper. His minder wasn't hearing it either. A muscular tattooed man in his mid-thirties sat as few seats away reading a motor cycle magazine. Black skull and crossbones T-shirt, scabby black jeans, combat boots and no conversation.

So Naylor ploughed through the *Sunday Mail* and the Scottish Supplement to the *Observer*. Both were killing him.

Inside the *Sunday Mail* there was an indignant piece about the public and private behaviour of lawyers. There were also two choice colour pics from his night at the Maltings. Naylor sighed. It had just been a matter of time before they surfaced. The trial opened tomorrow so they had it timed to perfection. In fact he found the pictures quite funny, which surprised him considering the down side.

No way would he ever be 'respectable' now. 'Nice' people would never choose 'that kind of person' for their solicitor. The local Tory Party would never select him as a candidate. His chances of becoming a freemason were about equal with him walking on water.

The *Observer* was an altogether more serious matter. Andrew Mackenzie was exercising his arithmetical abilities. He was investigating what relationship there might be between Naylor, National Security and SB Services. Smart boy, he'd traced Naylor's military record and was making a big thing of his history with Army Intelligence. Adding things up but careful not to spell out the total. Wasn't actually saying Naylor still spooked on the side, just ladled suggestion on thick. But the real damage was to SB Services. The journalist had dug up, from God knows where, some interesting stuff about their recent history.

Just before a big German brewery bought into the Scottish whisky industry it had hired them to dig up some dirt on the directors of the targeted distillery. There was evidence of blackmail and illegal phone tapping. The latter made Naylor's accusations against them much more credible. In any event the unravelling process had begun. The house of cards that was SB Services was set to tumble.

Banked up but under control, the furnace of anger still blazed hot in his brain, still left him bright eyed and crazed. This game, this chase had almost run its course. Tomorrow it would be over but those fires, he knew, would go on burning him away, consuming him little by little. Maybe one day it there'd be nothing left but ash and he'd be one of *them*. It almost happened on Friday night with

Haggerty.

Granada, the television people, had left a message on the office answering machine. They were probably after an interview. So no doubt World in Action would be featuring John Daniel Naylor in a some future exposé. No point in avoiding the interview. Be frank and open and completely cooperative. Oodle on the charm and tell them bugger all about anything but SB Services.

Over against the wall was a long sofa with two sleeping forms. Annie Burns' sister-in-law had gone but the boy was still there, changed out of the school uniform into a green and white Celtic track suit (was Annie a Pape?). Beside the boy was a thin bony faced man, obviously her younger brother.

Annie Burns' coma was in its fortieth hour. The doctors weren't so sure any more but weren't hopeful either. They just described her as "stable".

'Uh?' The minder grunted and nodded to Naylor's left.

Coming through the swing doors into the waiting area was a large familiar figure in a charcoal tweed coat, face rain damp and scowling. Two hard men on either side. These wore Next suits but Naylor could read the type a mile away in the dark. Especially in the dark.

He felt blood rise, surging in his throat. Here was somebody to kill, to clean off the face of the Earth. Big Bill Nicholson. Naylor had never before realised how arrogant, how aggressive the man seemed when you penetrated that professional, avuncular veneer. He strode up and stood, arms behind his back, dripping on the lino.

'Naylor.' Speaking as if to someone met casually in his club. Non-commital, pleasant almost.

CHAPTER FIFTEEN

Naylor sat there and looked coldly into the eyes, the big hard bloodshot eyes. 'You don't look so good, Bill. Take a seat.'

'There's some outstanding matters to discuss.'

'Bet you went to hear Jessye Norman on Wednesday, Bill. Hear the *Salome* piece brought the house down, eh?'

'I think it politic that you step outside and leave your little friend here.' The same measured Richard Burton tones.

'Sit down. I'm not going anywhere and neither are you.' Naylor nodded to his minder. 'Believe me if he doesn't want you to go, neither you or the Thomson Twins over there'll reach the door.'

'There are police downstairs, Naylor.'

'Then sit down before I kick you in the balls and the cops come bouncing in here by the dozen.'

'I don't think you realise – '

'I realise,' he barked, 'Oh I realise everything. Sit down!'

Looking round to see if the raised voice had attracted any attention he sat and waved his companions to do the same.

They moved round behind Naylor's minder and took a place on either side of him. The minder swung round to face them. He picked up a battered holdall from the floor and put his right arm inside and stayed like that.

'That's Alec, by the by. I suppose you might call him my personal security specialist. Now, I like to be up-front about things so I'd better tell you something. See that in that big bag on his lap there? Well, inside it there's a pump action shotgun. He got it in there by replacing the

214

butt with the handgrip from a revolver. Really ingenious, no?'

The two heavies stiffened, their eyes magnetised to the bag.

Naylor took a big slow breath. 'Listen, this is very important. If you or either of those two clowns of yours try anything smart they're instant spaghetti fucking bolognese and you're next on the menu. Is that perfectly, utterly and absolutely clear?'

Both heavies nodded slowly and slightly. Nicholson didn't flinch. Naylor almost admired that.

Nicholson said, 'We have to talk about SB Services.'

'Well, you've come to the right man, Bill. 'Cause I bet I know more about them than anyone alive, including themselves.'

Nicholson spent a moment absorbing the words. 'Haggerty has told you about the Study Group?'

Naylor slowly shook his head. 'No, I don't need Haggerty anymore. Yesterday he handed me everything he stole from them. Masses of very interesting printout, memos, faxes, contracts, diaries, client files … Oh, you name it, I've got it.'

'How …'

'Blood on the streets, Bill.'

'Ah. I see. Well, about the Study Group report …'

'You mean *Clawback* ? Want to talk about that, do you?'

Nicholson clasped his hands, closed his eyes and nodded. 'That and another matter …'

'Wonder what that might be? You realise I'm living a blackmailer's wet dream? SB Services were handling sensitive databases for all sorts of people, police, even Special Branch, drug squads, anti-terrorist units, vice. You know I have the names, addresses and signed statements of rent boys who've fraternised with certain Law Lords? Dates, times, places – the works. And as for the upper echelons of the Crown Office? Some of those out of town saunas are *so* popular. The photocopied credit card slips are wondrous to behold. Isn't it really heartening to realise that this is the sort of thing privatising public services leads to? More opportunities for the entrepreneur! All this information in the one set of computers? And backed up with a whole lot of incredible photographs. But that's not your number one worry is it? No, the real thing fluttering up your nose is Kromar. Right? SB Services is responsible for all aspects of Kromar security and you want to know how much Haggerty ripped off?'

Nicholson nodded. Then he cleared his throat and asked, 'Do you have any idea how much information he, er, sorry, *you* hold on the proposed nuclear reprocessing plant?'

'The process patent details. Plans for the Rathlin and Clydeholm proposed sites. Listed names of people known to be "sympathetic" in the Scottish Office, the SDI, Strathclyde Region, etcetera etcetera. Information like that must be worth a hell of a lot, Bill?'

'Well yes, there's already a vast sum invested, Naylor. It's a completely revolutionary reprocessing technology, two years clear ahead of the rest of the field but it's only a matter of time before the French build something similar, perhaps even bigger and better. We've already lost a terribly large sum because of the problems that arose in Ulster. This time it must go through.'

Naylor said, 'Didn't you realise that Haggerty couldn't care less about your bloody plant? There's no political capital for him. He wants an independent communist Scotland. He can only use what's of value for the 1992 election. By that time the plant will be public knowledge. And he hadn't the resources to run a blackmail operation on you. He couldn't see past *Clawback.*'

'That hardly alters the sensitivity of the situation today.'

'And you thought I was going to introduce this stuff as evidence in court? Thought Haggerty was jerking my strings? Thought I was going to say SB Services had killed Beattie to get the plans from her? Eh? He never gave her more than a couple of photocopied sheets on anything. Just to whet her appetite.'

Nicholson shrugged. 'It could still be a potentially damaging blow even if you were to lose the case.'

'Oh yeah. Even if your tame advocate managed to sit on it you mean? Even if it didn't come out in court I might still leak it to the press after the trial? Eh? Official Secrets wouldn't apply. They'd pick your bones clean. And good old Kromar's name would stink.' A thought sparked in Naylor's mind. 'And you've figured out just how much it would stink. Right? You've costed it. Right?'

He could see Nicholson squirm under these wee flashes of insight. It gave him joy.

The big man nodded. 'You're quite correct, of course. We estimate a drop in share price that could cost Kromar a great deal over the coming year.'

Naylor whistled. 'So you thought you'd drop by and give me another wee encourager, hmmm? Well, no. Better think again. Bill.'

'Oh no. Quite the contrary.'

'Contrary? What's the contrary, Bill?'

'I've been asked to make you an offer.'

'Tell me more. One I can't refuse?'

'One we hope you won't discard without reasonable consideration.'

'You interest me strangely.'

'The Kromar board has ordered me to offer you, on the understanding that all the sensitive information we've discussed, the material in your possession, remains strictly confidential ...' He had to swallow hard and draw a breath ... 'offer you a partnership, a senior partnership with Munro Kerr Meikle.'

Naylor shivered suddenly, uncontrollably.

'A senior partnership?'

Nicholson nodded.

Naylor began to laugh. 'First the shite and now the sugar, eh?' He laughed and laughed. Tears ran across his face and through the stubble on his chin.

'There's also a potential defence of your position re the MoD and the peace camp. We can also smooth over any trouble which may emerge regarding your position re the Law Society. In return for all of this we require the material Haggerty stole from his ex-employers. All of it. You have it nearby?'

Naylor just grinned.

Haggerty's fabulous treasure was secure from all of them. And not nearby. In the attic of a certain highly respectable "cottage" in Rhu. In the hands of the one person left on this unstable planet Naylor could trust with anything.

He said, 'It's perfectly safe. And any deal that goes down includes pressures on the Disciplinary Tribunal to get

218

me off the hook. I come out of that encounter lily white. As insurance you get the stuff back afterwards, say by Christmas, so long as I'm still practising on a full certificate. Free and clear. Right?'

'Agreed but I need an answer tonight. Obviously.'

Naylor shook his head. Too easy. Far too easy. 'No, Mr Nicholson. More. There has to be more.'

'Er ... Well, a supplementary cash settlement ...'

'How much!'

'One year's salary in advance. Fifty thousand pounds.'

'A hundred!'

Nicholson swallowed again. Then nodded. 'Very well.'

Naylor's heart battered with lust and rage.

'Just a couple of little extras ...'

He sighed. 'What extras, Naylor?'

'Details. Just finicky details. I want things put back together again before we proceed on this matter.'

'Put back together? I'm afraid I don't quite understand.'

'Get my typist back. Get Annie Burns' legs back.'

There was a small silence. 'Those unfortunate occurrences are beyond reclamation. I'm afraid you panicked SB Services into making an error of judgement with that bomb.'

'An excess of zeal, eh?'

'If you could come down to my car. The papers are there. Read them at your leisure. But we must have a signature tonight.'

Naylor stood.

'Tell you what I'll settle for.'

'What?'

'Your head on a silver platter. Has to be silver to go with the brilliant coif job, Bill.'

'Are you coming?'

'I don't mean figuratively. I mean it literally. Physical decapitation. Get the head to a taxidermist. Bob's your uncle. Now I'd want it by a week tomorrow to put in the office's new window.'

'Naylor?'

'Tell them they can keep the money so long as they kill you.'

'This conversation is totally unproductive. Are you coming down to sign or not?'

'Maybe I'm thinking about it …'

Across by the entrance to the ICU both Annie's son and her brother were awake and staring at them. The man had his arm around the boy.

The doors of the waiting area bumped open and two men staggered in, men in donkey jackets, faces streaked with gore. They were followed by two big men in studded leather jackets and a woman similarly dressed.

'Say they're old pals o' Mr Naylor's. They were in the back of that guy's car,' said one of the men, addressing Alec and indicating Big Bill.

One of the men in the donkey jackets was bleeding from the groin. He slumped to his knees beside Nicholson, white faced, gasping, bloody hands pressed to the ripped crotch of his jeans. Both the heavies who'd come in with Naylor stood. Alec and his holdall rose with them. The woman winked at Naylor.

'Naylor, this man is seriously injured,' said Nicholson alarm starting in his voice.

220

'So it was all ready and waiting down in the car for me was it Bill? And just in case I'd any trouble making up my mind you brought along my old pals here? Eh? '

'No! Jack, it's not the way it looks. Not at all. The offer is perfectly valid. Really. Please. You must believe me.'

'Must I? No, I don't think I must. I don't think I must at all.'

'We can make it more, if that's what you want. We can – ' He broke off as the wounded man keeled over onto the floor. 'Good grief, we'd best call a doctor for this chap.'

'What? For a big macho tough-guy like him? Naw. He wouldn't thank you for it.'

'But this man is bleeding uncontrollably.'

'Then let him bleed a while longer.'

'My God, Naylor,' rasped Nicholson. 'What have you sunk to?'

'Your level. And remember, if I'm in the clear after that tribunal, you and SB Services get a nice present from Santa. Otherwise the excrement impacts on the air conditioning.' He turned to Alec. 'Could you get them all out of here? Dump them somewhere?'

Alec nodded at the three others, then turned to the two well dressed heavies and motioned with the bag. They didn't budge so he pulled out the gun and gut whacked one with the muzzle, turned the butt on the other's face.

'And just a word to the wise before you go, Bill. Remember and be really safety conscious when you're getting into your car from now on. You and the rest of your partners at MKM. And pass the word to your dapper little chum the Colonel as well. Motoring's a lot more hazardous than ever these days. Can't be too careful. One mistake, one wee oversight and that's it. You're butchermeat, baby!'

Nicholson was cool again, holding together. He looked Naylor up and down and said, 'Mix with scum long enough and you become one of them!'

Naylor said, 'I know, Bill. It happened to you,' and blew him a kiss.

Sixteen:Largo

'NONE OF US APPRECIATED your gang of motor cycle thugs turning up at noon on Saturday, Jack. We did have people over from the Faslane camp. There was a demonstration scheduled, a major event!'

Debs Mooney looked totally out of place in Naylor's favourite Saltmarket café at half eight on Monday morning. Perfumes of hot fries and dank cold clothing clung in the steamy air. Thick-coated, anoraked, gloved and scarfed the breakfasters crammed into the room's narrow booths drinking, clattering cutlery on plates, bantering with waitresses who shouted through the kitchen hatch. Oval dishes piled with sizzling stodge were plundered eagerly. Instant coffee was spooned from an open topped bin in the hatch. The result was thick, black, heavily oxidised and undrinkable but the bacon rolls were classic. The tea was Co-op and reliable.

She wore a smart grey tweed coat over a pastel blue wool culotte suit. Sugarless weak tea sat unsipped in a glass mug before her.

'Listen, Debs, if they hadn't biked out there and babysat you lot there'd have been some other visitors turning up, a lot less pleasant. Some desperate and very dangerous visitors looking for something they'd lost. You don't have it. But they're not the type that's easy convinced. You'd have had your major event then alright. Believe me.'

'Who?'

'The people who compiled that little lot.' He leaned across and tapped the three photocopied printout sheets the Angels had delivered to the camp on their visit. 'Familiar, is it?'

She glanced at the sheets. 'There's a good deal more than Lexie Beattie had, but I imagine its the same material. Probably from the same source.'

'And after she read it she was happier about you?'

Debs shook her head. 'Not particularly. I'm sure by now you realise that what she read privately to me out at the camp were the details of my fiancé's death. Oh, if she was of the opinion that I was an IRA activist she'd have been quite content. She was a militant romantic. Not that she'd have ever supported any direct violent action herself. It was just the concept of an oppressed people struggling to be free which excited her so. I think this report just made me a little less unacceptable to her.'

'So its true, then?'

'All lies, Jack.' Pushing the papers across the table, she shook her head. 'In fact its worse. There are truthful elements in it but they've been warped to fit someone's paranoid fantasy.'

'Like what? Like your IRA boyfriend?'

'Disgusting. Repellent. Oh he certainly was a Republican. He was also a pacifist. At Oxford he spoke wonderfully in the Union debates against the use of violence as a solution to the problems of Northern Ireland.

224

Of course these people,' she nodded at the sheets, 'really, deep down, they never believe that there is such a beast as a pacifist. They assume small time pacifists to be simple minded idiots and the big timers to be the enemy in a surreptitious guise.'

'But your man just happens to wind up in the middle of an SAS ambush?'

'The hurley team massacre? Correct. Three men on that mini-bus died. Two of them were Provos and the three that escaped were also Provos. None of the others ran. They hadn't a clue what was happening so they kept their heads down and were captured. They're still in prison.'

'Really? According to this they were all Provos. Suspects before the ambush and convicted terrorists after it. That mini-bus had thirty automatic rifles and two thousand rounds of ammo concealed in the false roof.'

'I doubt if any but the Provos were aware that the bus was transporting a cache of arms from Coleraine to Armagh. Had they realised, they would certainly have made alternative arrangements. But the Provos had no intention of telling them. Travelling with a well known committed pacifist was such good cover after all.'

'And what about your father?'

'You mean my family, rather. What does it say?' She lifted a couple of pages and scanned them. 'Yes. *The Mooney family has long been involved with Irish Republican movements. The 1903 analysis by the Special Branch of the Royal Irish Constabulary traces these activities as far back as October 1791, when Percival Mooney helped Wolf Tone establish the Society of United Irishmen. Mooney was also instrumental in the French pro-Republican invasions of Ireland in 1796 and 1798.*

And that is it. On the basis of one ancestor's activities my whole family is branded in perpetuity. He's not even a direct ancestor. He was a cousin. As for my father, he is an academic. He has no political convictions worth talking about. I believe he used to vote Liberal but we don't talk much. When we do, we quarrel. Generation gap and all that, I imagine.'

'I'm supposed to believe you?'

She shrugged. 'Your beliefs are your own concern, Jack. Not mine.'

He said, 'Why the change of clothes? Where's the combat jacket gone and the CND stickers and the jeans?'

'I'm going home. That's Oxford by the way, not Cork. After digesting the reading material you despatched me I feel I have to do some fairly basic thinking.'

'About what?'

'I've spent years of hard and frustrating, sometimes heartbreaking work trying to establish a pan-Euro peace organisation. Now, well ... they've perverted it. Dirtied it all. So everything I've done has been to further the power of the Provos, has it? Just to back a Troops Out of Ulster campaign? Funny, I thought my prime concern would be the little matter of scrapping nuclear weapons from the Atlantic to the Urals. But if this is what the British Secret Service believes about me I'm sure the other European security organisations have similar files. No wonder its been such an uphill struggle. My values require complete re-examination. After all they have been used against me. What I must consider is to what extent I have been manipulated and ... by whom. I have to straighten all that out in my mind. Presently I am less than confident that my efforts, my struggles have been worthwhile.'

' "Twisted by knaves to make a trap for fools"?'

'Kipling was a lackey of Empire. Hardly relevant in the circumstances.'

'Is that a fact. But what do you really need to figure out? I'd have thought it'd all be fairly obvious now?'

'Betrayal is a bitter draught, Jack. I always face my enemies. Perhaps I was foolish to expect them to return the courtesy.'

'Naive, credulous, foolish? Does it matter? I mean that's the kind of person you are. That won't change. At the end of the day when you've done all this soul searching and great agonising and so on you're still going be one of those people, the poor dumb trusting shmucks that are always there. You know, the ones everybody can rely on to stand up and be counted. And knocked down like skittles. Right?'

'Its possible. And one day I may even be back.'

'Really? Even after all this? There's just no getting through to you is there? Let me spell it out in plain English.' He sighed and pointed through the grime wiped window at crowds huddling under a blaze of sleet, at the smeared lights of cars and buses. 'That is the street. And these days its a very very dangerous place!'

'It always was, Jack Naylor.' Debs said standing, hoisting a slate pigskin bag to her shoulder. She smiled. 'Just ask Lexie Beattie.'

Bending slightly, she kissed him on the lips and walked past the two large men in black leathers out to the door. An umbrella popped wide, dipped forward with her into the brume.

He was left with a dying whiff of floral scent.

'Bad news, Alan. Its time for the Section one-oh-two.'

The Glen Douglas campers had clubbed together to buy him a suit for the trial. It was an off-the-peg Burtons model in dove grey which fitted surprisingly well. Seeing him in it Naylor could more readily envision him in uniform, the dress uniform of a captain in the Parachute Regiment. The big man sat on the wall bench in a High Court cell looking puzzled.

Naylor said, 'I can't represent you. You'll need another solicitor. However MKM does have a junior partner upstairs. Right now he's drafting various documents with the third rate counsel they slipped on me. Don't try the big bluster and threat bit you did before. Now, I've got protection. Anyway, nobody's going to listen.'

He snapped open his briefcase and pulled out a sheaf of photocopies. Banks stopped, his eyes attracted to them, fascinated. Naylor said, 'Now, here's a wee surprise, Alan.'

As he held them out Banks snatched them, began reading, scanning each page rapidly.

'Yeah, thought they'd look familiar. Just like the ones you found in her house, eh? Yes, you're in there all right. It's a Friends and Enemies file. Alphabetical list of every operative actual or suspected who's active and in the field in Scotland, their affiliated organisations, personal details and so on. Debs Mooney's in there too. And, as you knew all along, so am I.'

Banks began frantically tearing the sheets.

'Don't be an idiot, Alan. They're photocopies. I have all the original printout safe and sound.'

He gaped at Naylor, looked almost as though he were about to burst into tears. Then he sat back down.

With a little, almost chagrined, gasp the man leaned back, his eyes closed. Naylor decided he looked more pensive than worried. What was he thinking? Trying to find a loophole? An escape clause? Some new legalistic ejection seat to rocket him through the High Court roof to freedom?

Banks said, 'Goodbye, Naylor.'

'And that's it is it?'

Banks opened his eyes.

Naylor said, 'Just "Goodbye, Naylor", eh? After all that garbage about how you needed someone like me? A person you could rely on? Someone you could trust to put the boat out for you, eh?'

'Why don't you just go away, Naylor?'

'Now, I'm going to give you my impression of how it was supposed to happen. I'm bound to get some of the details wrong but I think I've got the general idea right. Stop me if I go off the rails. Okay?'

'I'm not interested.'

'I guarantee you'll be interested. Absolutely guarantee it.'

'Oh really? Well hurry it up, will you?'

'Why? What's the big rush? You've all the time in the world, Alan. About fifteen years, ten with remission, I'd say.'

Banks' eyes met Naylor's. Cold and steady. Then he shrugged.

Naylor said. 'I wondered now and then why you didn't seem worried about any of this. Now I know why. You expected to be found guilty. It was part of your plan from the start. Right? There was to be the trial with me totally demoralised, making a complete cock-up of the defence notes, instructing some third rate counsel with the track record of a slug. And you'd go down, convicted but so surprised, pleading innocence and so on. Right so far?'

'Oh, sure. Off to prison til well into the next century. Just what I've always wanted. You should be writing science fiction, friend.'

Naylor smiled and wagged a finger. 'Ah, but then – and only then – someone, probably some journalist or other, would discover my links to the intelligence community. You'd make sure of that, Alan. You were aware of them the moment you read that file in Lexie Beattie's flat. Right again?'

Banks just looked bored.

Warming to his exposition, Naylor continued, 'The result – public outcry, an investigation and demands for a retrial. But with any jury in the country quite convinced you'd been totally stitched up, any trial would be a farce. They'd simply let you stroll off, free! A hero. An international example of victimisation. Famous. And then you use your magic to get Debs Mooney's Euro-peace network off the ground and you're in there. Right at the heart of it, the worm in the rose.'

The big man just gazed back in silence.

'Then you could have redeemed yourself, Alan. Right? Then your masters would have wanted you back again. Then they'd have been sweet, attentive, oh so grateful. Were they the ones who suggested how to salvage your career after you topped that medic in the NATO exercise? 'Course they were. Christ, there's always bound to be a place for the truly zealous. Right?'

There was a smirk now on Banks' face. He said, 'You really think you've got it all tied down now. Don't you?'

Naylor frowned and said, 'Tell you what I think. I think they suggested you might try your hand at intelligence work, go undercover and keep an eye on that fanatic Mooney and her Provo pals for starters then start digging deeper. Right? Keep your commission on the fly. And a nice fat salary from the Home Office. And of course she was so vulnerable too. They shot enough holes in her boyfriend to make him look like a string vest. So you moved right in there, Banksie? Couldn't have been that difficult, eh?'

'You leave her out of this!'

'My God and she thought you could walk on water! It must have been some blow to find out she really was a pacifist, that she was about as much an IRA terrorist as a half pound of Kerrigold butter!'

'So they were wrong about her. Are you close to finishing?'

'Humour me a minute longer. That was bad news but there was worse to come. Oh boy, was there ever. After all those boys down in Whitehall were looking for results, fresh info smoking hot from Ulster. Well, you're the man of zeal, no? But you could come up with what? Zip. So who else on the fringes might be a good mark? Someone they'd told you about? Maybe warned you about. Steer clear, eh? Never could resist a challenge? Lexie Beattie. They'd certainly have mentioned her. And the minute you realised Debs Mooney was a waste of time you started cosying up to the old woman. Visited her. Got her interested in the camp, in your anti-nuke plans? Right?'

Banks sighed, 'You're doing the talking.'

'But it was a bad move. She was far too wise for the likes of you. She was an old hand at the chase. Lexie really could run with the fox and hunt with the hounds. They'd told you she was a hazard to navigation, eh? Steer clear, eh? So … you never told them, did you? Bad move. You lit the blue touchpaper but forgot to retire immediately. Bang and did you ever get a big surprise.'

'Is this going to take much longer?'

'That day she came across to the camp and brought those sheets with the official dope on Debs. That was it! Boy, that must've really curled your hair. You'd heard it all before. Even though she skipped the IRA stuff and just read out some family history, you knew you'd heard it word for word. You knew she was quoting from the same file you'd been shown, right?'

'Really smart, you are, Naylor. Oh, God, what wouldn't I give for a brain like yours. Remember to leave it to science, won't you?'

'And if she could dig that up on Debs what might she dig up on you, eh? All your details available to her? The fact you were the real F branch plant? Then the ball would've been right up on the slates. The game a proverbial bogey and your career, your life, scuppered again. Only this time there'd be no second chances. Not when the big boys down south realised your own stupidity, your own excess of zeal, brought it about in the first place. So you went out there that afternoon to get the file, or files or whatever information she had. Did you think you could bully it out of her? Frighten her? Lexie Beattie was old but she was tough as old boots. Slapped her about a bit Alan?'

'Shut up. I've had you up to here. Now clear off!'

'Got rough?'

'Leave me alone, you stupid little grub. Get out!' Banks stood, loomed.

But Naylor was riding his horse to hell and nothing

could stop him now. 'Got zealous? Then you got excessively zealous again, didn't you? You killed her! Then you tore the place apart like a wild man. And hooray, you found it. A stack of photocopies. You read them. And this was the stuff alright. You read them and you found out about me. Then you burned them in the kitchen sink.'

'Of course in my shoes you'd have done it different, I suppose?'

Naylor said, 'But when you killed the old woman they realised their precious Captain Banks was out of control, eh? Another excess of zeal? They realised they'd made a bad mistake in you, Alan. And they decided to cut their losses. You were to go down for the crime, do your full fifteen years and be scrapped.'

He was crying. Banks was actually crying. 'It'll happen to you to. One day you'll be in the bloody corner, back to the fucking wall. And you'll behave like an animal, Naylor. Oh yes you will, you little toad ... you will ...'

Naylor went on, 'Was that when you got the idea about using me? Forced me to be your lawyer so when you lost the case you could expose me as a peace-camp spy? Then the big scandal and then you free as the proverbial bird. The fact I would be totally wasted, completely destroyed was just incidental, eh? Just too bad for poor old me?'

Banks was angry and choking, 'Know ... it all do you?'

'But by God I stuck with your case. Jee-zuz did I ever. Limpet. They tried everything to pry me off. Nothing worked. What a laugh. Me saving my ball and chain by jumping overboard. But it's all about to change.'

Tears balled down the big man's red cheeks. He was

shuddering, sobbing, sniffing. 'Don't know bugger all 'bout anything, Naylor. Wasn't my idea, you moron ... Was the plan! Always was the plan ... Even before I came ... Was what you were set up for. Years ago ... Not a *spy*.' He barked a broken laugh. 'Never were a *spy*. Just part of a plan. Expendable part. 'S why you were put in place. So some day there'd be someone like me they could put into the Euro peace movement. Plan was to martyr him. Big fake trial and he goes down. And then you'd be exposed. Sacrificial goat. He comes out smelling sweet. You tossed onto the slagheap. That was your only purpose, you idiot!'

'No!' Naylor shouted. It couldn't be. His brain, his ego raged against it. He tried to speak but Banks would not be stopped.

Through the shuddering and weeping his voice stormed relentless. 'Only I turned the tables on them, Naylor. You blind stupid bastard. Can't you see? Don't you realise what happened?'

Naylor felt shivers creep across the skin on his arms, across his shoulders and back.

Banks coughed and sniffed. He said, 'Plan went wrong. I really became one of them, Naylor. Me. Me! The Warrior ... sword into ploughshare ... became a believer. Believer, Naylor!' He threw his head back in a hard cracked cackle. 'Oldest story ... on earth, Naylor ... Fell in love, Naylor ... Fell for her. Love her. God, I love her. And Donnie ... Susan ... kids. Lexie was going to destroy it all ... was going to the *Record* with the whole thing about me and you ... everything ...would've destroyed it all ... all ... '

For maybe a minute Naylor sat there frozen. He was trying to readjust his psyche, like retuning a television to pick up a better picture.

The words echoed, 'Sacrificial goat ... not a *spy*. Not ever a *spy* ...'

He looked at the big man and felt a pity strong and as physical as hunger, as toothache.

Then he said, quietly. 'I've shown this Friends and Enemies file to the Judge, Alan. Told him it came into my hands on Friday. That the information contained therein on me is false but that I have to withdraw from acting. He agrees. There will be an inquiry but I have a suspicion I am going to be the one who comes out of this smelling of roses for once. Then I'm going to give a copy of this to the Crown. Not all of it, you understand. Just carefully selected extracts that will include only you and some other carefully planted blooms. Me. But not Debs. There's been enough blood and dirt smeared over her as it is. And, for what its worth, I'm sorry, Alan.'

He closed his case and lifted it, turned and banged on the door.

Behind him Banks was making a squeaking sound. 'love 'er ... really ... really ... love 'er ...'

'Aye, I know Alan. I know. Its rough. How does the song go again? *Life's a bitch and then you die ...*'

Seventeen:Coda

COMES A TIME even Mother Theresa runs out of social credit. The dealers had laid on protection until the case was over, so Naylor started paying his team of hired muscle the afternoon he came out of court. Three fifty a day plus expenses that brought the total to nearer five hundred. That's it, he reckoned, pay them off tonight, bung them another couple of ton for a party and it's back to long sleepless nights with the lights all burning.

Anyway there was only so much Guns and Roses he could take. It almost surprised him his hi-fi so used to Klemperer and Pavarotti could play heavy metal, didn't rebel. Not that he said anything. No, no, they were fundamentally good guys after all. The music was just a wee bit of light relief. Well deserved. Sort of.

The abrupt turn around at the court the previous morning had caught the media short. The drama was played out and Naylor gone before they snatched a whiff of it going down. They just watched the short mechanical farce of bald admissions submitted by counsel and Banks being shackled to a life sentence.

The phone went back on the hook today. One day

off was enough after all he needed business. By five o'clock there were twenty two messages on his answering machine. He'd sit at the kitchen table listening to them as they phoned in. Eight client calls including three new clients, two on indictments. And journos wanting interviews, an actual solicitation to serialise his memoirs, SB Services with an improved offer for the return of their stolen treasure, Nicholson saying he felt confident the Disciplinary Tribunal would come to nothing. But still not a word from Paul Goldman. A call from the hospital ...

It was Annie Burns' brother.

Naylor snatched up the receiver and asked how she was.

'Oh, hello. Er, well Annie's out the coma. Came out about half an hour ago. She's still no' conscious. Tell the truth she just looks much the same to me but they've got these wires stuck onto her heid that tell them if her brain's working and they say she's just sleeping now. Say there's a good chance she's gonny live. Thought you'd want to know.'

'Did they say when they think she'll wake up?'

'Sometime the night.'

'Is there anything I can do?'

'Well ... er ... '

'Yes?'

'It's a wee bit ... You know?

'What is it?'

'Well, I have to ... to find out ... You see me and the wife's looking after David the now ... And I was laid off in the summer there ... Look ... is there any money supposed to be coming to Annie, like her wages or something? I mean we're really up against it, man?'

238

'Oh, right. Well, er …. I hadn't thought about it. Is she going to be coming back to work?'

'Christ, I don't know.'

'Mmmm. Things are tight, you know? Look, tell you what. I'll be down there later tonight. Maybe we can discuss it then. Okay?'

'Fine. That's fine. See you then.'

'Right,' said Naylor and hung up. Money. Everything was bloody money. Everybody wanted a slice out of him. Cutting him to bits. The tightwad in Naylor was alive once more.

'Damnation.'

A partly filled in an application to join the Legal Defence Union lay before him on the table. Time, he decided, to take these kind of sensible precautions. If, that was, the LDU would have him. Now that might pose a few problems.

Beside the form was a pile of newspapers. He picked a couple and flicked through them. Saturday's *Evening Times* had a nice colour picture of Annie on an inside spread. She looked younger. The hair was darker and the eyes brighter. Almost pretty. Probably taken four or five years ago, he guessed. Funny how when she smiles the corners of her mouth turn down.

He worked through the rest of the bundle. A great picture of Debs Mooney in *Today*, coming out of court after the hang-glider carry on. That was the Debs he knew, sharp featured, big combat jacket and a pair of genuinely skin-tight jeans painted on to those great legs. Split at the knee. Made him smile.

Surprisingly, there was a big photograph of Lexie Beattie in that morning's *Herald* on the 'Perspective' page.

The picture startled Naylor. It showed a young, attractive woman at a dinner table. She was laughing. And laughing with her, looking at her, was the unmistakable figure of Hermann Goering.

Brian Wilson's article detailed the friendships this famous Scottish Nationalist had cultivated with top German Nazis during the thirties. But hadn't Flanagan and Rose given Naylor all the gen on that? Yes, about how Beattie had spied for Britain? Of course they had. But the more he looked into that face, looked into those glittering eyes, the less certain he grew. After all, he now knew she'd always played both ends against the middle. Look at those rings on her fingers. Always stacked the deck in her own favour. Look at that diamond necklace. Always loaded the dice ...

Well, hadn't she?

'Got company.' One of his minders killed the racket from the hi-fi and Naylor looked up.

Coming through the door, carrying a duffle bag and two bulging Safeway shoppers was Paul Goldman.

Naylor stood. 'Paul. Where've you been? I've been trying to phone you since yesterday. Ruth just keeps telling me ... '

But Paul Goldman's face was a rock, eyes bloodshot, skin pale. He dropped his burden to the floor. There was more than just Haggerty's mother lode from SB Services. There was all the gear of Naylor had accumulated at the Rhu house over the years. Naylor gaped at it, puzzled, confused.

'What's ... Er, what's the score? You all right?' Naylor said.

Paul Goldman's voice was hard as his face, hard and grating. He said, 'I read it! Couldn't resist it. Read that printout. All that stuff about you in it … Stooge for the faceless men down in Whitehall. I couldn't believe that. No. Couldn't.' He paused, controlling himself. 'But it was true. Every damn word of it was true. Every word.'

Naylor sagged back to his seat at the kitchen table.

'Jee-zuz. I knew I should've told you.'

'How could you do that? How can anybody do that? Anybody?'

'C'mon, Paul. We all hide things from each other. I mean it's not that bad I – '

'You idiot!' Paul Goldman shouted. 'That's not what I'm talking about. You. It's you in their secret bastarding police. You working for the Gestapo all those years and years.'

'Surely – '

'Surely nothing! Jackie, Jackie. Don't you realise what I am? Did it never in all that time, those hundreds of drunken nights, cross your mind for one second what I am?'

'What you are? Look, pal, we've got to sit down and talk this – '

'Listen to me! Look at me! What do you know about me? About my family? Well, Herr Obergruperfuhrer!'

Then Naylor knew and the understanding breathed winter through him.

'That's right. I am a Jew.'

Naylor cradled his face in his hands. 'No. No. Listen Paul, it wasn't like that.'

'Moron. Don't you know yet? Its always like that.'

'No. Paul – '

'I don't have any aunts or uncles. Remember? I told you often enough, Jackie? My parents made it out of Europe by the skin of their teeth. My mother was caught by your people in Paris in 1941 – '

'They're not my – '

'They let her go. Some bureaucratic screw up. They raped her, you know. That sweet gentle woman. Oh, that's why I was so keen to give you all the support I could when I found out what had happened to you. Because I thought nobody deserved that ever ever ever – ' Suddenly his voice broke and he began pulling things out of the bags and hurling them at Naylor. LPs, books, boots. 'But. I. Was. Wraaaaawng ...' Coffee mug smashing on the table, framed picture of Naylor's ex-wife smacking off his shoulder.

One of the heavies casually threw a punch at the side of Paul Goldman's head knocking him to his knees.

'No,' Naylor shouted waving his hands, running round the table. 'No. Don't touch him.'

He tried helping the small man to his feet but he pushed Naylor away.

'Fuckoff! Get away.' He swayed and bent over, picked up his spectacles, broken, and staggered out to the front door. Naylor followed. 'Never want to see you again. Never. Die. Die and rot!'

'Paul, it's all over now. Honest. Over for ever. Everything's changed.'

Paul Goldman stopped on the stairs and glared up at Naylor. The flesh around his left eye was swelling and discolouring already from the blow. His lip curled as he spoke. 'You'll never change. Look at you, Mister Big with his gang of bully boys. No, Jackie Naylor. Once a dirty fascist bastard always a dirty fascist bastard.'

'But Paul, we're going to hear the Adadeus Trio. Right? Paul? Paul ...'

He paid them off. Gave them the extra couple of hundred. That pleased them. The big bearded guy who'd thumped Paul Goldman even apologised. They took their Guns and Roses albums and left.

Trying not to think he switched on the tele. The news was on BBC and Scottish. Some war criminal in Dundee was fighting extradition attempts. He switched off and tried a mantra. Repeat something meaningless. It stopped him thinking but the tension stayed. Just made him feel he was pumped full of helium. Bloated and floating but no, he felt heavy too, like some long drowned corpse.

After a while sitting in the room he decided it was time for some self-pity and popped Previn and the LSO's version of Barber's Adagio for Strings into the CD player. Turned the volume up and walked about the room for a few minutes, then into the kitchen.

The fridge was loaded with supplies, bacon, black pudding, cheese, butter, two loaves, half gallon of milk, half gallon of fruit juice and on and on. Freezer well stocked, meals galore, couple of garlic chickens, shoulder of lamb, two pound casserole all cooked and frozen and ready for resurrection in the microwave. No Absolut.

The cupboard. Two packets of Kenco individual coffee filters, Brooke Bond Scottish tea bags, Nescafé Blend 37, corned beef in tins, chopped ham and pork, packets of pasta, jars of sauces, smoked salmon soup, chicken noodle, game consommé, pickles, tinned peas, beans, white sugar, brown sugar, sea salt. More and more and more. But what shall it profit a man that he gain the whole world, never mind a full larder?

Still, not so much as a can of export.

God. And this man needs a drink. Could always go

down the off-license. Get some rocket fuel from Metal Morag? Well … maybe tomorrow or the day after. Once his confidence was built up a wee bit.

Naylor cursed quietly and kicked the cupboard door closed. Then he opened it. There was a pair of scissors hanging from a hook on the back. Taking them he walked back to the living room. Again he looked at the papers spread out on the table.

It took less than a couple of minutes to cut out the three photographs and sellotape them to the wall.

Debs Mooney. Lexie Beattie. Annie Burns.

The three women in my life, he thought. One gone. One dead. The other half dead, crippled for life.

And to top it my best mate hates the very idea of me.

Suppose that has say something about Jack Naylor.

Outside a wind was rising, drawing giant cloud fists together in the black city sky. Putting out the stars. Suffocating the moon and smacking the first insults of rain across the tenements. In the street below two of the fluorescent lights were out and one pale and dying.

Time passed and still he sat there, still looking into their eyes, Debs' sharp, Annie's bright. Those eyes could open all sorts of little doors inside his head. And did. They were more than unforgettable. They wrote the sort of memories into your blood that lived with you till the second you died.

Like Lexie's Beattie's eyes, which had never looked back into his own.

And the voice of Paul Goldman.

END

NOWLEDGEMENTS
FOR
)ODING MR NAYLOR.
tion and support; Dorothy Pieri for her
rice, Frank Pieri for suggestions, Ken
rs, the partners and staff of Mullane and
ition and patience, Donald Saunders,
lasgow Herald Library staff (Auntie,
e, Stroma, Kath, Bev, Maris and Jane),
Wullie Coffey, Ian Bruce, Doug Gillon,
Jack McLean, Ron Anderson.

ny own. No prizes for spotting them, ok?